FALLING FOR THE BOSS

THE GREAT LOVELY FALLS - BOOK THREE

ALIE GARNETT

For my Family

MEET THE LOVELY'S

Sera Lovely – 35-year-old who is the Director of HR, stepmom of five, mom of two but loves them all equally, engaged to Harrison Dean

Nelle Harper Lee Lovely - 30-year-old who is a Personal assistant to a jerk, CEO/CFO/just plain C of Lovely Catering with Lucy and boss off all her sisters. (and anyone else she wants to boss around)

Mabel Lovely - 28-year-old who is a twin to Lucy, Children's Lit professor, married to Clifton Scott V.

Lucy Lovely - 28-year-old who is a twin to Mabel, works for Lovely Catering and Cleans offices.

Agatha Lovely - 26-year-old who is an amazing artist and mediocre bartender looking for a job.

Buzz Lovely – 25-year-old reporter for the times, youngest and more outgoing of the big girls (Psst: if you have a lead on a good story, Buzz needs a break)

Emmaline Lovely – 15-year-old sullen teen who likes her life without a father present.

Violet Lovely – 8-year-old upbeat, outgoing artist who loves having a dad for the first time in her life.

CHAPTER ONE

"I JUST WANT to be a mistress. You know, rock his world and then let him go home to the wife and kids and let me read in peace. Don't laugh."

The blonde in the booth behind him at the bar was telling her friend about the jobs she thought that she would be good at. The first was parole officer, and the second was mistress. The second was way more interesting than the first. As she was calmly telling this to her friend, she shelled peanuts from the bowl beside her, only to pile the nuts on a napkin, not even eating them.

Kaine Hawthorn's attention was immediately drawn to her words. Not just the words, but the entire conversation. Though she hadn't recognized him when he'd walked past her and sat down, he instantly knew who she was: his quite subdued morning personal assistant. Yes, he had two of them: tired, dull Nelle, and mousy Christine. One in the morning, and one for the afternoon. His days were usually sixteen hours long or longer, and one personal person wasn't enough. So, a year before, he had added Nelle in the mornings.

If his executive assistant hadn't put her foot down on him working twenty-four hours a day, he wouldn't need two. Recently he had been thinking of adding another assistant but hated to even think about training someone new.

He had always assumed she had a live-in boyfriend and kids. She was Miss Lovely, after all, and she constantly looked tired. After a year, he thought she'd be used to the early morning hours.

Finding her in this bar had been strange. It was a run-down dive bar, miles from work. He would never have come here except he found an article online that the Grog was one of the top twenty-five bars in the city. From where he sat, he saw that was a lie. And it seemed everyone already knew that because the place was dead—even with a live band playing.

Most of the time, he was too busy to even be in the bar at this time of night, but tonight was special. Tonight, he needed a drink, and drinking alone at home didn't seem like any fun.

"You don't read," her brunette friend reminded her.

"That's because I spend all of my time with Grant. There's no time to read. Now Yvette, with two T's, can have him. I am so over the whole boyfriend thing. He was over all the time, even when I wasn't there!" Nelle complained loudly.

"I know. I live there too." Her friend's voice showed no doubt she was tired of it.

"I'm so glad I didn't move in with him. I would have lost my bedroom and been on the couch," Nelle said, making them both laugh.

"How are you going to become a mistress? There's not much call for that anymore. Now, in Victorian England, you'd be snatched up in a heartbeat," her friend said wistfully.

"Really? You're going to talk to me about Victorian England? Today?" Her voice had a trace of lecturing in it.

"If I said Paris, would you be happier? You don't have time to be a mistress anyway. You have a job that takes up all your fun sex time, reason A that Grant found Yvette." Her friend argued.

Kaine couldn't help but wonder why her job with him would interfere at all. She was done at noon every day.

"What's reason B?" He could see her face from memory, questioning him in the past. The woman had never been afraid to question him, unlike nearly all of his employees.

"Wandering cocks wander," her friend replied, making them both laugh again. Kaine wondered how much they had already drunk tonight.

"Why did I let him back in after he nearly had sex with Julie in our house? Nobody gets to have sex in our house but us. That came out wrong." Nelle giggled.

"It's true. So, are you going to take out an ad looking for a man in search of a mistress? A mistress with bad hours?" her friend asked. She was giggly too now.

"I think it would only attract weirdos. Do you think there's an app for it?" Nelle questioned.

"I think weirdos would be on that also."

"I'll just have to give up on it then. Maybe in my next life." She laughed again.

"Lucy and Cliff are at the Fish. It's Agatha's first day," the brunette said.

Nelle slid out of the booth. "Let's go. This place isn't doing it for me."

Turning to make sure it was really Nelle, he caught sight of her familiar ass. Tonight, it was encased in blue denim, but it was the same ass he saw every day. It was a very nice ass. Her friend's wasn't half bad either, but Nelle's was the better of the two.

For over a year, he had appreciated that ass. Usually, it was in black slacks, sometimes in a black skirt. But always in black. Sometimes, Nelle's pants were oddly dirty, and black shouldn't look dirty. Sometimes, he could smell food permeating from her. It wasn't bad, just not what you wanted in an office.

Tonight's jeans and a soft T-shirt were a change; a nice change. She looked more comfortable and relaxed in street clothes. Less tired than usual. Or maybe she was less tired because it was only ten at night and not four in the morning. Her being up this late might be why she was always so tired, even if was Friday night.

When he had first met her, his executive assistant, Bex Carter, had already hired her, so it didn't matter what he thought. Bex didn't care if her long blonde hair was gorgeous or that her brown eyes were always upbeat, even when she was crabby. And she could be crabby—she was in a bad mood at least twice a week.

Never had he suspected that she was giggly. It was possible she was only giggly when she was drunk. Either way, he liked her giggly and drunk. Better than the quiet and moody attitude he usually got for eight hours a day.

But now he had seen it, and he liked it. Now he just had to find a way to convince her that he was exactly what she needed. Because she was exactly what he was looking for in a mistress.

CHAPTER TWO

"NELLE," came the disembodied voice from the inner office. Looking up as she slid off her raincoat, she saw the door was closed, but she knew he was there. Apparently, she wasn't going to get a moment to herself before her day started, even if she was almost half an hour early. What she wouldn't give for a few minutes of alone time. She should have just sat in her car for a while in the parking lot.

"I'm taking off my coat, Mr. Hawthorn." The intercom might be shut off, but she said it anyway. He wasn't even supposed to be here yet—it wasn't even 4 a.m.! He should be sleeping, dreaming of how to make her life miserable for another few hours. But then again, why dream it when he could live it?

"Now, Nelle." He pronounced the E at the end; he always did, and she always hated it. Not that it usually mattered how it was pronounced since she had always gone by Harper, her middle name. But she had been blessed with the name Nelle Harper Lee Lovely at birth, so here at work, she was Nelle. At her other job, she was Harper again, but there she was her own boss, so she could call herself anything.

"Coming, Mr. Hawthorn," she said again to the closed door,

putting her wet raincoat in the closet she kept her possessions in during her eight-hour shift.

Opening the door, she hurried into the inner office. Kaine Hawthorn was alone. He was behind his desk already working, and Harper couldn't decide if he was still up or already up. His dirty blond hair was a mess, but it always was, as if someone had just run their fingers through it.

If it had been later in the day, Bex Carter would be with him. Bex disliked Harper immensely and had told Harper that over the last year many times. The feeling was mutual. The black-haired woman was usually creeping around wherever Kaine Hawthorn was, but she arrived at work at 8 a.m. and not a moment earlier. How she got away with that, Harper didn't know, but since Bex was one of Kaine's favorite employees, she had some idea.

"Sorry, Mr. Hawthorn. I had to take off my coat. It's pouring outside," she explained as she sat in the chair across from him. She quickly checked for Bex to be lurking around despite the hour and was happy she saw nobody.

"You're late." Kaine's blue eyes looked down at her, even though they were sitting directly across the desk from him. For some reason, he always had a way of looking right down his perfectly straight nose at her.

"Actually, I'm early, Mr. Hawthorn. It isn't even 3:40 a.m. I start at 4:00," she informed him, tapping her pen on the paper she held.

Not that she didn't want to be late. In fact, she didn't want to be there at all, really. She wanted to be in her bed. She glanced up at him, grinning to herself as she wondered what he would be like in bed. He was looking right at her, and her eyes slammed back on the paper as an unwelcome heat spreading through her body.

Getting her mind back to the present, she wanted to inform him she was almost always early. Every time he had been there when she was, he claimed she was late, and it used to bother her. Not today, though. Today she was exhausted and had just wanted to nap at her desk until he showed up closer to eight, a normal time for people to work. But Kaine Hawthorn was not normal, which was why he had two personal assistants. He also had Bex, his executive assistant, who worked normal hours, or so she assumed. But Harper's shift was over before noon, so she'd never been in the office then. What was the point of hanging out there?

"I like my employees to be punctual," he replied, looking down at his desk, ignoring her.

"I am." Harper knew she was back talking, but at this point, she didn't care as she stared at the top of his head. Four in the morning was not her best time. Talk to her at closer to 4 p.m., and she was sweet as pie, or as close as she ever got to it.

"What did you say, Miss Lovely?" His blue eyes snapped up to hers.

Okay, so maybe she shouldn't have said it, but it had been a year of this. He was always in a bad mood when he showed up before her shift began, always. It wasn't her fault he was here, and he didn't need to take it out on her.

"I said, I *am* punctual. My hours are four to twelve, and I was here before four." She didn't add that she had gotten up at 2 a.m. to get fifty pounds of chicken marinating for the dinner party she was catering that night. Or that she would have been late if her sister Agatha hadn't stumbled into the house as she was getting the chicken ready and helped her out.

"Maybe I should move your hours to three to eleven." He leaned back in his chair, smiling as if it were the best idea he had ever had.

"Then you would have to change Christine's to eleven to seven. At that point, you should just think about adding another assistant for the missing eight hours. Then you can have someone here twenty-four hours a day, and you would never have to stop working." She wrote "jerk" on her pad, then added the word "chicken" in case he ever saw it. Then she quickly "jerk" anyway.

"That's a thought." He looked her over again. "Is that shirt clean?"

Looking down, she saw her formerly sky-blue shirt was not so much anymore. Her apron hadn't done its job, and there were most likely chicken splatters on her chest. Raw chicken and very noticeable splatters.

"It was when I put it on. I must have gotten something on it since then," she mumbled, pushing her blonde hair back behind her ears, realizing she forgot to put it up today.

"Could it be something with lemons? I suddenly smell lemons."

"Possibly." Possibly not!

There were ten lemons in the marinade, and she had cut them all this morning, but it looked more like chicken. And to her, it smelled like chicken—raw chicken. "Where is Bex?"

"Home, I suspect," was all he said.

"Okay. What can I help you with this fine early morning?" She mocked her stepmom's ever chipper personality, but her humor was lost on Kaine Hawthorn.

Sera was the one who had found this job for Harper a year before. Sera worked a few blocks down and was the HR director at a law firm. Apparently, she knew about job openings all over downtown. So when her stepmom had learned Hawthorn International was looking to fill a personal assistant job for the oddest hours ever, Sera thought of her. Harper couldn't work eight to five and needed something to pay for the kitchen upgrades that were needed to take their catering business to the next level. It was taking forever to get enough money for that.

"I need someone who can take care of my personal life, including parties, dinners, and keeping my home staff in line." He got up from his chair but didn't take his eyes off of her. Coming around the desk, he finished, "And making sure that when I'm *not* working, everything is taken care of."

Her eyes were on him. Kaine never left his chair as they discussed anything. The only time she saw him out of the chair was when he was leaving the office. She didn't know if she liked him walking around the office for no reason.

He leaned against the desk and unbuttoned his navy suit jacket, which left her eye-level with his crotch. Not that she was complaining, just observing.

"Doesn't Bex do that for you?" Harper looked up at him, pulling her eyes from where they had wandered. He was tall when she was standing, but when she was sitting, it was even worse. Today she realized that she liked this blue suit better than his black ones. It made his eyes bluer, that's all—no other reason.

"No, Bex takes care of my professional life. I need someone like her for my personal life." Those blue eyes were boring into her, making her slightly uncomfortable.

Blinking up at him, she wondered what he was really asking. He had no personal life, and as far as she knew, he was always at work. After all, it was four in the morning right now, and here he was, already at work.

"Okay, good luck on finding someone suitable," she offered. She had no clue who would want that job or why he was even talking to her about it.

"Do you have children?" His question caught her off guard. He had never asked before. Why would he care?

"No," she responded in confusion.

Kaine folded his arms. "Why not?"

"Because of this amazing little invention called a condom. You should look into it." She didn't just say that to her boss, her sexy-as-sin boss whose dick was in line with her face? What was she even thinking? What happened to *"I'm single and don't want kids yet"*?

Cracking a smile, he said, "I've heard of them. Were you at the Grog on Friday night?"

She knew her face showed as much shock as she felt. Was he having her watched? Why would he do that? Or had he been there, sitting at a back booth reading reports, staring at his computer and on his phone? How could she have missed that?

"I might have been. Why?" She folded her arms over her chicken stains.

"I want to hire you."

"For what?" she asked warily, trying to remember her night with her sister Mabel. What had they even talked about? Some she couldn't remember, some she did, but hoped her boss hadn't heard any of it.

Between drinking a lot that night and all the family drama of Mabel getting engaged to her twin sister's best friend the next morning,

Harper had learned a lot and forgotten most of what had been said at the bar.

"Mistress. I want you to be my mistress." He wasn't grinning anymore. He wasn't doing anything but looking at her. Arms crossed. Analyzing her.

"I don't think I'm qualified for that, Mr. Hawthorn." Her mouth had gone dry. Sure, she had pictured him naked over the last year, many, many times. But he almost always had a scowl on his face even while naked.

"I think you're more than qualified, Nelle. You're a good personal assistant, which would make you good at keeping my house in order." His eyes met hers. She was sure he was aware she wasn't a good personal assistant. Mediocre at best.

"Oh, mistress of the house. How Victorian of you. I still don't think I'm qualified, and I really don't have time to run your household. I really don't know what your household consists of, but I'm sure I don't have the time," Harper knew she was rambling.

"Nelle, this would be a business arrangement. I would pay you handsomely for your time." Kaine uncrossed his arms and slid his hands into his pockets.

"More than I make now?" Her eyebrow went up in question.

She did need more money. She had a kitchen to remodel but no money for it. So far, they had limped along with the kitchen at the house with some minor renovations, but if they wanted to grow their catering company, they needed a more commercial-like kitchen. That would take money—money she couldn't raise fast enough as a personal assistant. Sure, Lucy, her business partner and sister, worked as a waitress at a bar and cleaned offices, but that was even worse for making money quickly.

"Substantially more. But you would be my mistress in every sense of the word." Pulling his hands from his pockets, he gripped the desk behind him.

"Every?" Was he talking about sex?

"*Every*, Nelle. You would be sleeping in my bed." He confirmed her suspicions.

"Do you even have a bed?" Whoops. That wasn't what she wanted to say. "I mean, what if I have a boyfriend?"

"I don't share."

"For how long? Not forever." Her mind was racing. Sure, she could sleep with him; her mind had done it tons of times. But could her body?

"A month. After that, we decide if you want to stay. You attend every function I attend, you sleep at my house, and you make sure everything is running smoothly there."

"I'll need two nights off a week, and I say what nights." Sitting up straighter, her mind started racing. With the nights off, she could still do events and not have Lucy do everything, though Lucy would have to do more than she did now. But it was only for a month.

"Two nights in seven days? I can do that, but not the nights I have events."

"And days. I get every day off from ten to seven. Everyday." That would give her time to make the food the nights she had to 'work.' "You don't ask where I am or be possessive. I'm a free woman."

"As long as you remember that I don't share and that you are mine, do what you want with your time," he agreed, face still blank.

"I won't forget, don't worry. I need thirty thousand dollars." She knew she wasn't worth that, but that was how much an amazing kitchen remodel was worth. It was the amount of money they were trying to save up.

"Deal. I'll draw up a contract." He didn't even blink at the dollar amount.

"What? A contract?" Had she just agreed to this? What was she even thinking? Shouldn't she think about it a bit more?

"This may be personal, but I want everything legal," he informed her with a smile as he pushed off his desk.

She leaned back in her chair and analyzed him. "Why me? You don't even like me."

"I don't dislike you, Nelle. You just have no ambition and are questionably good at your job." Kaine said as he went back around his desk to sit in his chair. Back to his normal place.

"But you want me to take care of your house?" Did he really think of her like that? No *ambition*? She had two fucking jobs! One she owned and spent every waking hour thinking about.

"My house is small and easily managed. I'm sure you'll get used to bossing people around."

Harper took the dig as a compliment. She was the oldest of seven girls; she was born with a bossy side. Growing up to be a temperamental chef didn't help. She had more than one shirt that said "Boss" on it.

"You don't even know if we're compatible in bed."

"We will be." He merely smirked. His confidence was astonishing at times.

"When would I start?"

"Today. I'll have Bex find you a replacement."

"Bex? I suppose I'll have to see her constantly. Why didn't you just ask her?" Harper rolled her eyes.

Kaine's executive assistant was gorgeous: willow-thin and could wear a pants suit like she was born in it. Though her dark hair was too short for Harper's liking, she always had it styled perfectly. If it were up to Harper, she would have chosen the other woman over herself, even if she was always a bit more opinionated than necessary.

"Because she's not my type, and her wife wouldn't approve," he said with a straight face.

Harper could have smacked herself. Of course, the woman was married, which was a bigger surprise than that she was married to a woman. That poor woman!

"I'll do it if I get half the money upfront."

"What if it doesn't work out?"

"I'll make it work, Mr. Hawthorn." She could get the kitchen done by the end of the month, completely done and ready by the time it was over. This was what she needed to put Lovely Catering on the map.

His eyebrow shot up at her statement. "How do you know we'll be compatible in bed?"

"Because that kind of money makes me wet. Never mind the face behind it." Her mouth got away from her again.

"We'll see if I can make you wetter than the money can." He pushed off the edge of the desk and walked around it. "Get to work, Nelle. I'll need you here until my lawyer shows up with the paperwork. After that, you can be done for the day."

Getting up, Harper had no idea what to do with four hours before she officially became his mistress. What did one do in this situation? She had a few things to do, and none involved doing a lick of work for Hawthorn International. She had a contractor to hire.

CHAPTER THREE

After watching his soon-to-be-mistress's hips sway out of his office, he began typing an email to Harrison Dean. It was highly unusual, but the man wouldn't say anything to him about it. He paid him enough not to think.

When he had heard her tell her friend she was interested, so was he. Though he had thought she would end up declining, he was more than happy she had agreed. Now he got all the benefits of a girlfriend without the emotions they always brought into the situation. All he wanted was a woman on his arm for events and sex. No more being alone for either one for at least a month.

In reality, he had wanted sex from her since she had first walked into his office a year before. Even though her clothes were not her size or style, she had been gorgeous. Tall, long-legged, and blonde, with a sassy mouth to go with it. It had taken a few weeks to find out about her mouth. Usually, she was able to reign it in, but every so often, she let it go.

All year he had a hands-off approach with her. She never gave any indication she thought of him as anything but a boss, but he didn't think he gave any indication he wanted her either. It seemed both were on the same wavelength.

Was she only willing to be with him for the money? He doubted it. As much as she said the money was her motivation, he didn't think she was the sort to do anything for money—no matter how much.

For hours he had focused on work instead of her sitting alone out in the outer office. They were the only ones in the building except for security, but a mountain of paperwork got his mind past his thoughts of starting early to see if they were compatible or not.

Just before eight, his lawyer walked into his office unannounced. *I guess she's giving up on doing her job at all*, Kaine decided as Harrison Dean entered the room.

"Harrison." He watched the man sit down in the chair Nelle had been just hours before.

"I typed up what I hope is a joke, Kaine." Harrison gave him a disapproving look. "Because someone who runs your house doesn't make this kind of money, nor do they work nights and attend functions with their boss.

"No need to question it, Harrison. This is between her and me. Are you seeing anyone?" Kaine grinned. Harrison had been both his friend and lawyer for years. The other man's ex-wife was friends with his ex-wife. Their friendship had survived and grown after their divorces.

"I am. Actually, I'm getting married at the end of October. You'll get an invitation as soon as the wife-to-be gets the invitation list done." Harrison set the file he was carrying on the desk. It was green and stood out from all the white papers that were covering the service.

"Married? I thought you'd said never again?"

"I thought so too, but then I found Sera. She works in HR, and I asked her to come meet you since this was obviously a joke." He pointed at the file. "But her stepdaughter needed her to run an errand right away."

"A stepkid that she does errands for? You don't even like kids," Kaine reminded him. They had that in common. Neither had wanted kids nor had kids. He had a nephew, and that was as close to kids as he wanted to get.

"The stepkids are as much her kids as her biological ones. She has two—I mean, we have two. The two that are actually Sera's are mine. One is fifteen, and the other is eight."

That took him by surprise. He had known Harrison and Veronica had gone through difficulties in their marriage, but that he had cheated on her? That was new.

"What does Veronica say about a kid born while you were still married?" Kaine knew that Harrison had only been divorced around five years, just like him.

"She couldn't even speak for a while, especially when Sera told her that her eggs were a toxic environment. Then Veronica tried to spread around that I had cheated on her, but it just made her mad that nobody cared anymore. It's been years."

"Sounds like Veronica."

Harrison tossed a green file folder on his desk. "So, back to this. I don't even know if this is legal, but it's on paper, and once it is signed, you'll have whatever you want to call it."

"I call it 'girlfriend without emotions.' The dream." Kaine pickup up the file and leaned back in his chair. It was the perfect plan.

"Sadly, this woman will also have emotions, and it might be worse than an actual girlfriend."

"Girlfriends want marriage. This contract says nothing about marriage." He held up the papers.

"Women sometimes don't work like that. Emotions happen despite whatever you two have agreed on," Harrison said, nodding at the contract Kaine was holding.

Reading through them, Kaine was happy with it. Everything discussed was in the file, right down to her demanded days off. He hadn't thought of her wanting personal time when he had thought up the plan, but she was right to need time away.

"Let's get these signed." He grabbed his phone and punched the button for his personal assistant. Today was the perfect day for this since Bex was in late this morning. Bex couldn't stand most of the staff.

The phone went unanswered. "Was she out there when you came?"

"Who?" Harrison turned to look out the door.

"Nelle. She isn't answering."

"No, it was empty out there." Harrison turned back to him.

Without a word, Kaine went out to see where she was. The office was empty, so he went out into the hallway, where the office was coming alive as the day started. Checking the break room, there were a lot of people loafing around, but not Nelle.

"Who are you looking for, Mr. Hawthorn?" a woman whose name he couldn't remember asked.

"Miss Lovely. Have you seen her?"

He was starting to think that she had changed her mind and was gone. Or in HR complaining about sexual harassment. Which it was.

"Last I saw, she was in the bathroom." She nodded down the hallway.

"Thanks," he called as he headed for the room. No, he was not allowed in there, but she was needed in his office. This needed to get done right now.

Slamming into the room, he was glad she was alone—and glad she was wearing just a bra. She quickly spun away from him, but not fast enough for him not to catch a glimpse of what he was going to see tonight.

"What the fuck! This is the lady's room." He watched her pull a gray shirt on. The blue one was at her feet.

"You were missing." He watched as she pulled her blond hair from below the shirt and let it cascade down her back.

"I was here, not missing. My mom brought me a clean shirt since you were so concerned earlier about it." Turning, she picked up the shirt and slammed it into the garbage can. Her new shirt was still unbuttoned, giving him more glimpse of her breasts and flat stomach.

"The papers are here to sign." He couldn't take his eyes off her as she buttoned her new shirt.

"Oh, fucking *joy*." She tucked in her shirt as she grumbled.

"Don't sound so excited, Nelle." He tried not to grin at her sass.

"Gosh, I'm just so excited, I don't know what I'm more excited about! Telling the maids how to clean your underwear or getting into them myself," she said in a fake southern accent as she walked past him.

Pulling her to him before she left the bathroom, he whispered hoarsely, "It had better be getting in them yourself."

Her body was soft and warm, and he held her a moment too long before letting her go. When he did, she pushed off him like he was the enemy. He hoped she changed her tune because her attitude didn't bode well for the next month.

CHAPTER FOUR

Harper left the bathroom and hoped he stayed behind as she went back to her office. Why he had needed to barge into the bathroom, she had no idea. It was her mom's, so it was tighter than Harper liked, but it wasn't covered in chicken fat.

Stopping at her desk, she watched Kaine walk back into his office. She could see the back of his lawyer's head. She had seen him a few times in the last year, but not in months. Not that she paid much attention—her focus wasn't on this job after all. This one had always just been a way to make money for her actual career.

Gathering her courage, she walked into the office and closed the door behind her. All she had to do was sign a paper, and she would have her kitchen. Okay, there were a few other things she wanted, but those came later. Out of sight, out of mind.

"Harrison Dean, this is Nelle Lovely," Kaine introduced them with a wave.

Harper almost passed out on the spot. Her mom's fucking fiancé?! How could Kaine's lawyer be her mom's boyfriend? She hadn't even remembered him when her mom had introduced them a few months before. Of all the lawyers in this town, it had to be him.

"Miss Lovely." He held out his hand with a fucking grin. Yup, he knew who she was. But for some reason, he wasn't mentioning that they knew each other, just like she wasn't.

They had only met a few times, and along with her he had met her four sisters those days also, but he remembered her. Not that she had a conversation with him or spent any one-on-one time with him, but he seemed to know her. No way was he not telling her mom on her. And she would kill her.

"Mr. Dean." She took his hand and shook it, her mind racing on how to get out of this.

"Can I talk to Miss Lovely for a moment?" Harrison asked, pulling her to the far corner of the office as Kaine watched.

"Don't lecture me," she stated firmly.

"I don't have to; you have a mother for that. But what the fuck?" he hissed. She had never heard him talk like this, but once again, they hadn't had too many conversations.

"I have my reasons. And don't be so fucking pious, Harrison. Remember, I know your fiancé better than you do. I don't even think you know how much she talks. Oh, and need I say *couch baby*?" she whispered.

The sudden red tint to his ears said she'd hit the right nerve. That his and Sera's youngest was conceived on a couch had recently come to light, and the teasing hadn't stopped yet. Harper hoped it never would.

"That was not my fault," he hissed, but it took two to tango, and he was one of the two. The only thing that wasn't his fault was that he had been unaware of his daughter until recently.

"I know what I'm doing. Don't tell my mother," she demanded quietly, though, in reality, she had no idea what she was doing. She was probably going crazy.

"How are you going to explain living with a man?"

"I won't. They'll never know. I'm not moving out." No way was she losing her room because of this.

The house rule was that if you slept more than five days away from the house, your room went to Buzz, who currently slept on the couch. Their house was one bedroom short.

"I know the terms, Harper. It's Harper, right? What the fuck is Nelle about?" He looked down at her.

"It's Nelle; silent E. Long name, Harrison. We all have long names. Nelle Harper Lee Lovely. How can I get you not to tell her?"

"We have no secrets, Harper," Harrison insisted.

"Let's see, last week she didn't drop her phone. She threw it at Buzz." Harper stated, suddenly hating her stepmom's suddenly squeaky-clean life.

"*Real* secrets," Harrison said.

"She was engaged once. Bet she didn't tell you that!" Harper leveled him a stare.

"Twice, actually, but that's beside the point. I will keep this for a month, but after that, you're on your own. It had better be worth it," he stated.

"It's so fucking worth it." She rubbed her hands together, then stopped. It looked weird.

After breaking their huddle, they went back to Kaine's desk. Harper picked up the contract and looked at it. Not that she knew what she was reading at all or even cared. As long as she got the money, she would do anything, even what it said in the contract.

"Do you two know each other?" Kaine asked, looking at them as Harper flipped to the next page. Two pages? It could be covered in three words: sex for money. Lawyers made everything complicating.

"We have a mutual friend. Shouldn't be an issue since my part in this is very small," Harrison replied and pointed to where everyone should sign.

Harper signed her life away for a month without the hesitation she'd thought she would have. She was crazy to even think about signing it, much less doing it. She was actually signing a paper saying she would be fucking this man for a month. The rest was just fluff.

With one last glance at Harper, Harrison took his copy of the contract with him as he left, leaving her alone with Kaine for the first time since they had agreed to have sex legally. They were alone, and she had no idea what to say.

"What now?" she bit her lip as she looked anywhere but at him.

"You can clean out your desk, and I will see you at seven. My place." Handing her a copy, Kaine took his copy of the contract and put it in the file cabinet.

"Ten. I'm busy today until ten." She argued with the contract still in her hand. Was this a breach of contract? She had no idea, but she couldn't leave Lucy high and dry the first day. The chicken was to be served at 6:30 p.m.

"Contract says 7:00 p.m." He lifted it before dropping it into a folder.

Harper stared at the drawer and wondered which file it went into. Was there a file already made for this? Had he done this before? Wouldn't Harrison have told her if he had made this contract before?

"Tomorrow will be seven. Tonight is ten. I could do nine in a pinch." She bit her lip. Lucy would have to take everything home.

"Eight." He turned to her.

"*Nine*. I will try for earlier, but it probably won't happen." She folded her arms. She was never getting out of there by eight.

"Are you going to be in breach of contract the first day?"

It *was* a breach of contract! She knew it. She could have been a lawyer.

"No, but I have a previous commitment. You can work another hour this way. You love work anyway," she pointed out.

"Nine then. But don't be late."

"Traffic is traffic, Mr. Hawthorn." She headed for the door, hoping she could keep her eyes on the clock tonight. She already knew she was going to be late; fourteen hours wouldn't be enough to get everything done.

"Kaine," he called after her, "You should start calling me Kaine, Nelle."

"Just Nelle. The second E is silent." She was out the door before he could answer. Not that it mattered that he said her name wrong. It was only a month after all.

CHAPTER FIVE

"DID your morning personal assistant not show up?" Bex asked as she walked into the office at ten, nodding to the empty office she had just walked through.

"No, she'll just be working in another area for a while," Kaine hedged. Bex had been with him for too long not to tell her, but he was going to try. Until today he had no secrets from her, or so she thought.

"She wasn't very good. I'll find someone to fill in for her until we get a replacement. Where did you put her?" Bex sat down, still typing on her phone. The top of her head was all he saw, and her short black hair was the same style she always wore. It was short enough that he could see the silver earrings that ran up her left ear. The other only had one stud in it. For years, her entire life had been on her phone, but she was efficient with it.

"She'll be taking care of my household." He put his pen down, turning all his attention to the woman in front of him.

Bex looked up at him with one dark eyebrow raised. "What does that mean? I've been to your house, and it takes an hour a week to get it taken care of. She's an awful personal assistant, but she's better than that. Maybe just a little. What will she be doing all the time?"

"Attending functions and such." He leaned back in his chair.

Instantly, her dark eyebrow went up again. He knew the look; he had gotten it before. Bex was on to him.

"The 'and such' isn't legal." Bex tried to hide her grin as she put her phone on the desk and glared at him.

"It's all legal. Nothing to worry about." He had made sure of it as best he could. There was nothing in the contract about sex, just everything else. The sex was implied.

"Are you paying her?" Bex's brown eyes were judging him.

"Yes, she has a job to do." No way was he telling her how much. Bex would blow a gasket. The dollar amount Nelle had said was high, but he planned to get his money's worth from her, even if her office skills were lacking.

"Can I tell that to your sister? About Nelle's job? Because she'll automatically be thinking blow jobs like I am." Bex couldn't hide her grin anymore.

Kaine loved Bex working in his office; had for years. The woman was effective and efficient and could almost read his mind now. But her being his sister's wife sometimes was just too much. Whether she was telling Arabella everything he did, or Bex was telling him way too much about his sister's wants and needs, it was too much.

"Mind out of the gutter, Bex. Don't tell my sister anything. She doesn't need to know." This was a perfect example of the inconvenience of his executive assistant and sister being married. Very inconvenient.

"Because when she asks over supper what her big brother is up to, I'm supposed to not tell her he's paying for sex." Bex tried not to giggle but failed.

"Talk to her about the shop, or her pregnancy, or the weather. Leave me out of it. And I'm not paying for sex; I am paying her to make sure my personal life is as organized as my professional life."

"And sex?" Bex added with a smile.

"Just drop it. You won't have to see her here anymore. Focus on that." They had many discussions about Bex's dislike of Nelle. Not that it ever mattered to Kaine; she did her job.

"Why her? You can have your pick. Sure, she's cute, but really,

Kaine? She's not *that* cute."

"That is my business, Bex. Mine."

"Touché. She doesn't look like Claudia at all. All this time I thought you Hawthorns had a type." Bex grinned at him. Since both Claudia and Bex shared dark hair and dark eyes, they looked similar. But everything else about the women were completely different: body shape, personalities, style, sexual preference. In the end, they were completely different.

"I don't want to talk about her, ever," he stated and frowned at her. She had crossed a line, one she was well aware of. Claudia was not to be talked about.

"Okay, I'll drop it. But Nelle? There are so many hot women who work here, Kaine." Her eyes instantly went to her phone as a blush spread across her face. She'd realized what she had said, and suddenly, it was she who was seeing the inconvenience of being married to his sister.

"Nelle," he corrected the pronunciation for her. "The last 'E' is silent."

"Sorry. I've been saying your girlfriend's name wrong for a year. But then again, it's her fault for never correcting me." Bex stood up. Her phone was back in her hand, and she was typing something. He hoped she wasn't texting his sister.

"She's not my girlfriend. That's why I'm doing this. I don't want a girlfriend, just everything a girlfriend brings to the table." He watched her go, knowing that the chair outside his office would be filled within hours.

It was true that Nelle looked nothing like Claudia, who had been dark-haired and short. Nelle was a tall, leggy blonde. Maybe he needed the opposite of the woman he had promised to love forever—a promise he was still keeping. It didn't matter that she was now Mrs. James Horn, and had been for three years. It didn't erase the dozen years they had been together.

This had nothing to do with her. This was about him and getting his needs met without a commitment. He had been married once and thought it would last forever—he didn't want to do it again.

CHAPTER SIX

"A PERSONAL ASSISTANT? At his house? Are you even qualified for that?" Lucy asked as she dumped another twenty pounds of potatoes in the sink to peel.

Though two years younger than Harper, Lucy was far more laid back than her sister. Over the last year, she had gone from being a reliable waitress to her right hand. So much so that Harper didn't know how she would have made it this far without Lucy.

"Yes, I am. I've been a personal assistant for over a year," Harper replied. She was now completely covered in chicken fat and didn't care at all as she laid them out on a pan to bake.

"At his office, not at his house." Lucy scrunched up her nose, and Harper didn't know if it was because of the idea of working at some guy's house or if the long brown lock of hair that had escaped her ponytail hours ago was tickling her.

"Same thing." She shrugged, pretending that the two jobs were interchangeable.

"But you hated it," Lucy reminded her.

"And I'll hate this also. But in a month, I'm done, and we'll have a new kitchen. I mean new appliances and countertops and even that fridge we've been eyeing." Harper tried to get her off the subject of her job and on to more important things, like the kitchen, which was the entire reason for the job.

"Why is he paying you so much?" Lucy asked.

Harper knew she should have lied to her sister about the amount of money she was getting. Lucy wasn't as dumb as she always pretended to be, but she had undiagnosed dyslexia, which meant she couldn't read well. For Harper, that meant she never wanted to do the books, so hiding the money would have been easy. Except she told.

"Because I work all the time he isn't at work. What's the point of having a personal assistant for your home when you're not there? I have to be there when he is, so it's what I'll do."

"Can't he be alone?"

"He doesn't want to. He wants someone to make sure the maids do their work, and the chef is making him the right stuff. And other stuff he needs done." Moving on to another pan, Harper thought about making shit up to tell her sisters about her new job.

"Do you have to sleep with him or just sit by the bed and watch?" Agatha asked from the table where she was eating cereal and, until this moment, just listening. She didn't do raw chicken—Harper had asked many times.

Agatha would be the perfect helper for their catering company. She was the second youngest in the family and was an artist, but she had yet to make anything of it, which meant she worked waitressing and bartending jobs in the evenings and nights. She'd have plenty of time to help with the catering, but she stubbornly said no every time.

"I get my own room, but I'll be home enough to keep my room. Buzz can't have it." Harper stated firmly. Buzz was currently without a room, and Harper wasn't giving hers up, even for a kitchen. The house had seven bedrooms and eight residents. Buzz had moved out of her boyfriend's place over a year before, and so far, no one had moved out. And though both Maby and Sera were engaged, they had not moved out officially, maintaining a night in every few days. Sadly, Lucy's twin Maby brought her fiancé with her.

"Sounds fishy. You once said he was pretty hot," Agatha reminded her.

"He's okay, but this job gets us a new kitchen, and a new kitchen will give us more jobs. After a month, I'm quitting, and we can focus everything on our business. I'll find another part-time job after that," Harper explained as she washed her hands in the not-to-code sink.

"But you won't get to help all month?" Lucy tried to hide the worry as she asked. Harper knew it was a lot to ask her sister, but there was no other way. And it was just a month.

"I can prep during the day, and I get two nights off a week to do jobs. We can make this work. You've done it alone before," Harper reminded Lucy as she slid the pans into the two-small oven.

"I have, but I've always had you near." Lucy worried her lip as she concentrated a little too hard on peeling the potatoes.

"You can call; I just can't go anywhere to help." Harper hated letting go of the control she had of the company, but Lucy needed this. The diagnoses had caused Harper to reevaluate how much she let Lucy do, and she knew she had to let go of her tight control.

"Because she'll be having sex with her boss," Agatha announced as if there were more people than just Lucy and Harper in the room.

Glaring at her younger sister, Harper wondered if Agatha knew. Her black-haired sister was the "aware" one of the five. Dismissing the comment, she swore at her and got a laugh from the two. This was why she wanted to remodel the house's kitchen and not rent or buy some kitchen space somewhere—her sisters were here. Sure, Lucy would always be there, but she loved having Agatha, Mabel, or Buzz show up. Even the two little ones would sit with them and talk as they worked.

"I have to leave by nine tonight. I start right away," Harper said, hoping Lucy would remember later.

"Okay, I'll have Maby help me with cleanup," Lucy said about her twin. Lucy and Mabel were identical and sometimes they were hard to tell apart until you knew them, but they were polar opposites in personality and interests. Though Maby helped out some, there was no way she would want to cook anything. Lucy, on the other hand, could have cooked this entire meal without looking at a recipe.

"I thought Maby was busy?" Agatha was still at the table watching, her cereal long gone.

Since she had been engaged for like half a second, her sister was probably busy in bed with her fiancé. But Harper knew that Cliff would probably help out as well since he and Lucy were buddies. It might even be a good thing to have the twins work together for a night. They had been fighting a lot lately.

"She says she is, but she's not. She just doesn't want to help. But Cliff will make her; he's good for her," Lucy informed them. Maby never wanted to help. She usually pulled the "I have a job" card, which was true since she was a college professor. But she was never free in the evenings when her sisters needed her.

"Harper, have you slept since I saw you this morning?" Agatha asked, not moving from the table in case she was put to work.

"No, no time." Harper glared at her sister for a moment and wondered if she should ask her the same thing. Agatha had bags under her eyes that she hadn't had this morning. But the woman would just get mad and leave if Harper brought it up, so instead, she sighed and pulled ingredients from the refrigerator for hors d'oeuvres.

"You won't be able to watch your boss sleep if you pass out." Agatha got up and grabbed some cheese from her and set it on the counter.

"I'll be fine. I just need to get through this day. I knew going in it was going to be bad." She shrugged. It wasn't the ideal way to start a month of hot sex, but it was how it was going to be. At least being busy meant that she wouldn't have a lot of time to think about it. Or so she hoped.

CHAPTER SEVEN

BEX HAD FOUND a replacement for Nelle within an hour and was currently waiting outside his office. Kaine wondered if Bex had wanted to fire Nelle for a while.

It had been years since he'd been unable to concentrate on work, but images of Nelle's breasts were playing on repeat in his mind. That and the fact that he would be seeing them tonight—well, more than seeing them.

"Are you working late, Kaine?" Bex's grin was more annoying than the fact that he had forgotten he had requested the folder she was carrying.

"Yes. My day doesn't end at five," he reminded her.

"But now you have someone waiting at home." She giggled a little. He definitely should not have told her.

"Just drop it. My personal life is my business, not yours." He folded his arms over his chest. He didn't need this from her. Here, she was his employee.

"Kaine, you're quite grumpy for having a sure thing at home. I was hoping for you to be in a great mood right now. I would be. Hell, I am! But you're going home to Nelle, and I get to go home to Bella; sweet, sexy Bella." She grinned at him.

"I don't care that you put a ring on it, Bex. She's still my sister."

"I'm glad I got the cute one."

"Me too." He couldn't help but like his sister-in-law, even though she was a bitch in the office. At home, she was as devoted to his sister and their family as he had always wanted for his sister's spouse. The two were maybe a little too touchy-feely, but maybe in time, that would stop.

"I'm heading home to see the cuter Hawthorn. Need anything before I go?"

"No, you can go." He looked back at the pile of papers he needed to read before the end of the day. Most had been on his desk for hours.

"Thanks. I was going anyway." Bex walked out of the room.

Pulling up to his house just after 8 p.m., he saw a light shining in the entryway. It had probably been left on by the chef before he had left. As he walked in, the house was completely empty. There was food warming in the oven, and the house was spotless, just like he liked it. Hopefully, his newest employee could keep it this way.

With less than an hour before Nelle was scheduled to be there, he went up to his bedroom and made sure there was space in the closet and the dresser for her things. If she was going to live here, she would need room for her stuff. She had the entire day to pack to move in with him. If she happened to bring more than two suitcases, he would have to make some space.

Glancing around the room, he wondered what she would think of it. Claudia had decorated it years before, and the dark cherry furniture and black and white bedspread were not his taste. But so far, he hadn't thought about changing it until now. He should have had the head maid purchase something more colorful and modern, but it was too late now.

His watch told him it was ten minutes to nine; Nelle would be here at any moment. If she came at all. Sure, she had signed the paper, but that didn't mean she would come. No way was he taking her to court over the contract. They both knew that.

Kaine walked out to the driveway to wait for her in case she showed up. He stood in the dark, wondering if this wasn't his worst idea ever. After all, he had only worked with the woman for a year and knew very little about her. Now he was letting her move into his house for a month.

At five after, he was still waiting for her, still hoping that she was coming. It slowly dawned on him that he would probably never see her again. As he pushed himself away from the garage, he heard a loud, thumping car radio coming down his quiet street. In the years he had lived there, he hadn't noticed anybody having their radio too loud. Not that he spent much time outside his house.

As he watched, the gray Jeep slowly came up his street, the entire car thumping to the music. Oddly, it wasn't even teenager-type music; it was a familiar tune that slowly came towards him. To his surprise, the car turned into his driveway, pulling up to near where he was standing.

The car slammed on its breaks, and the driver sang as loudly as she possibly could in the enclosed car. The song was "9-5" by Dolly Parton, and when she said "bossman," Nelle pointed right at him. The relief that she had actually shown up was replaced by amusement at her choice. She shut the car off once the chorus was over, and the entire neighborhood went silent, except for her humming as she got out of the car. She reached back in and pulled out a backpack with a Smurf on it, then shut the door behind her.

"Made it!" she announced with a grin. "And you can pay for this."

Handing him a speeding ticket as she brushed past him on the way towards the house. Looking at the ticket, he asked, "Why am I paying for this?"

"I tried to be sharp, but Officer Hillman said no." She pointed at him and slung the bag over her shoulder. Tonight, she was wearing a red T-shirt that said "File End" in yellow letters. It made her look way younger than she had this morning. He knew she was thirty from her employee file, but he would card her tonight if he was bartending. "And if you don't pay it, Maby will be pissed. This is her truck."

"Where's yours?" He followed her, admiring that ass in black jeans tonight. Back in black. Tonight, her hair was in a French braid down her backside. He didn't think he had seen it in that style before.

"The house. Hers was in the back, so I took it. She can just take mine to work tomorrow," she explained and walked into the house as if she had been there a hundred times.

"Who may be pissed?" He shut the door behind them. Her explanation made no sense. "Do you have more bags?"

"No, just this. I'll go home every day, so I don't need much."

"Doesn't seem like a lot."

"It's enough. So, how is this going to work?" She looked around the house.

"Did you want to eat?" he offered. Even if it was late, it was an activity that seemed innocent enough. None of the other ones running through his head were.

"What are we having?" she wrinkled as nose as she asked.

"The chef made *Barigoule of Spring Vegetables* and frozen chocolate mousse for dessert." He smiled, hoping it wasn't too over-the-top for her. He had no idea what she liked to eat.

Making a face of annoyance, she groaned, "French? *Really*? You can keep your *barigoule*, but I will try the *marquise au chocolat*."

"You know French?" he was taken aback at her almost perfect pronunciation.

"Yes, it said so on my resume." She shrugged. "Four years in high school, and then I lived in Paris for almost four years."

Kaine just stared at Nelle for a moment. The woman had just sung to him about not letting her boss get her down, and now she had just told him she had lived in a foreign country for years, something he had dreamed of doing when he was younger.

"But you don't like French cooking?"

"Just tired of it still. Give me a pizza, and I'll be happy." She hitched the bag further up her shoulder.

"This way to the dining room." He pointed and walked towards it.

"Nice house. Do you live alone?" she asked as she followed.

"It's just me. I don't have any staff overnight," he replied, pulling out a chair for her in the big room.

Thanking him, she sat down in it after tossing her backpack on the ground. As she settled in, Kaine went into the kitchen to get the meals and dessert. Before he had the hot plates out of the oven, she was there in the room with him, backpack on again.

"Nice kitchen. Is your chef French, or did he just make something French tonight?" She grinned at him and slid a bowl closer to her to look at it, not seeming to care that the plates were hot as she moved them.

"French. His name's Philip," he said while watching her.

"Real French or just French taught?" She took a spoon and tasted the broth.

"Real French. I mean, from France." He took the other bowl and put it on the counter.

She pointed to the bowl. "Do you like this?"

"Yes, it's an acquired taste." He leaned against the counter.

"No, it is made wrong." She pushed it away and dropped her bag from her shoulder onto the stool next to her. "Too much fennel, and I don't think he put in any peppercorn.

"Do you cook?" He looked at her in surprise, then tasted it to see if she was right. To him, it tasted the same as always.

"I dabble." She gave him a half-grin. Fuck, she was cute when she did that.

"I don't know if Philip will let you *dabble* in his kitchen." He took a bite of the dish, feeling it tasted just like it always did.

"Then Philip may have to go on vacation for a while. I can cook for you." She pushed the bowl away from her again with the shake of her head.

"I prefer Philip."

"Then enjoy your bad supper." She pointed to it.

"I will. What does 'File End' stand for?" He looked at her shirt.

"No idea, but I like it." She looked down at it also. "Want one?"

"Sure." He slid his bowl to the stool next to hers.

"I'll grab you one tomorrow, but I can't guarantee red." She rubbed her eyes as she looked at his meal.

"Doesn't matter. Are you tired?"

"Yeah, just staying awake in the truck was hard. Until Dolly came on." She grinned at the memory.

Nelle suddenly jumped up, went to the fridge, and dug around until she found what she was looking for. Tossing the plastic dish on the counter, she shut the door with her foot and peeled back the plastic that covered the chocolate desserts.

She touched it lightly, then pushed harder and sighed as she pulled her finger out and licked it. "Amateur. These should be close to frozen. Not bad-tasting, though."

Watching her lick the creamy filling from her finger, he knew this had been his best decision ever. His cock was quivering at the sight. Everything about her was amazing, from the fact that she wasn't wearing a bra under the red T-shirt to the tiniest glimpse of a tattoo on the back of her neck.

"What's the tattoo of?"

Her hand instantly went to the back of her neck. "A harp. Stupid and ironic. Where can I put my stuff?"

He instantly slid off the stool and led her from the room, food forgotten as they went. Leading her up the stairs to the second floor, he walked towards the master bedroom. There was no turning back once they went through those doors.

She didn't hesitate as they walked in, just looked around as she had since she first walked into the house. "Can I take a shower? I'm all sweaty and gross."

"Sure, right through here." He led her to the master bathroom.

"You can finish eating, and I'll shower. Then I guess we *tremper le biscuit*." She dropped her backpack.

"What does that mean?" he asked as she started to unbraid her hair.

All she did was wink and turn her back on him.

Leaving her to shower and get ready, he headed back downstairs, but the meal had lost its appeal. After tossing everything out, he put the dishes in the dishwasher and wondered what she had been doing all day to make her so tired. They had both probably been up the same amount of time, but she had almost the entire day off.

After getting the kitchen organized and turning the downstairs lights off, he headed upstairs to his bedroom. It was just how he had left it not twenty minutes before, except now there was a woman in his bed—a sleeping woman, but a woman just the same.

She was sleeping on her stomach, and wet blonde hair surrounded her as she nestled into his pillow. The blankets had slid down her back, and he saw she was naked at least from the waist up. But completely asleep.

The lights were on, and the bathroom was a mess. As he cleaned up after her, he wondered if she was faking it, but she didn't move. Not when he started shutting lights down, not when he stripped out of his clothes, and not even when he climbed in beside her and pulled her into his arms. She just groaned and let her body slide into his as if they had been sleeping together for years.

If she was faking, she was very good at it.

CHAPTER EIGHT

THE ROOM WAS pitch black as the opening lines to "Manic Monday" came from Harper's phone. It was already 3 a.m. Rolling over, Harper groaned at the injustice of her life as she listened to the words. She was happy it wasn't Monday. Or was it? She had no idea what day it even was anymore, so she asked the room. Technology would tell her the answers to life.

Her computer voice assistant was silent in the dark room. She asked again, this time with a bit of anger the machine would never pick up on.

"It's Tuesday," came a deep voice from beside her, not even close to the female robotic voice she was waiting for. Not just any voice, Mr. Hawthorn's deep voice in the bed beside her.

Grabbing her phone, she turned off the song and flopped back onto the bed. Somehow, in less than twenty-four hours, she had forgotten everything. Or just forgot for a moment because she was starting to remember everything now. *Everything.*

Including the fact that she fell asleep before he'd returned to the bedroom. For half a second, she had been as ready as she was going to be, and then she was asleep.

"Sorry, I fell asleep. Long day," she said lamely. The shower took everything she had left out of her, or maybe just stole the last of the adrenaline that had gotten her into his house last night.

"No problem." She felt him roll her way.

"Did you enjoy your supper? Or did you finally realize it was bland? Because it was bland." As her eyes adjusted to the darkness, the little bit of moonlight was just enough for her to see him beside her. So close.

"My chef is excellent." His fingers trailed down her arm.

Trying to control the shiver that ran through her body, she whispered, "Shall we agree to disagree, Mr. Hawthorn?"

"We won't talk about it again. Right now, there are better things to do than talk." He kissed her shoulder, delicate, soft kisses that ran across her collar bone.

"You have to get up for work." Even as she said the words, her hands skimmed his shoulders and down his chest, feeling his silky skin and hard muscles as she went.

"I don't have to be there at four." His hand cupped her naked breast, and his thumb rubbed across her nipple, reminding her she was naked already.

She gasped at his touch and replied, "Sure, now you're all lax on being there on time. For a year, I had to put up with you as soon as I got there."

Watching him suckle her nipple, she tried to tear her eyes from it. Not that she wanted to as she ran her fingers through his unruly hair before a moan escaped her—a moan she couldn't control.

How he was able to turn her on so fast, she didn't know. She assumed it was in the contract, and she just hadn't read that part. She never got this hot this fast.

"Now you'll have to put up with me being here, Miss Lovely." He bit down gently on her peaked nipple.

"The things I have to put up with." Running her nails up his sides, she found muscles that had been hidden under his clothes all these months. Now she knew they were there and got to explore them in the moonlight.

"Your life is very difficult." He bit down on her other nipple, making her back arch.

"Thank you for noticing." Her hands slid down his sides, and she hooked her thumbs in his boxers to pull them down.

Moving his hips away from her hands, he said, "Not yet. I haven't spent enough time tasting you."

"Hopefully, I'm not as bland as your supper." That made her giggle until his hands sliding down her stomach made her moan in anticipation. Either he was very good at this, or it had been too long since she had done it.

Arching off the bed as his fingers slid across her clit, she gasped and grabbed his hips again. She needed him inside her now. But they were just out of reach.

"No." He chastised and used both hands to grab her wrists and pin them above her head. Looking into her eyes, he said, "Not until I say."

As his eyes were on hers, she grinned and used her body weight to push him off balance until he was on his back. The shock in his blue eyes made her laugh as she replied mockingly, "Not until I say!"

Shimming down his body, she slid her core over his still-covered erection, making him groan. His hands cupped her breasts as she scraped her nails from his chest to his boxers. As her hands were sliding under his waistband, he sat up and encircled her with his arms, taking a nipple into his mouth.

His arms were as tight as metal bands as he nuzzled, sucked, and bit, making her shake with anticipation. When he moved to the other, she moaned and cursed as his tongue swirled around the hard peak. All the teasing made her ache between her legs.

In an instant, she was back on her back, and her arms were stretched above her head. She was happy to let him do what he wanted—he seemed to know exactly what her body needed even better than she did.

"Not. Until. I. Say." His harsh words sent shivers throughout her body. She should have known he would be this demanding. But was he more demanding than she was?

"I say!" She wiggled her hips, demanding attention.

His eyes took in her naked body as if he were trying to memorize it, and the attention made her try and free her hands. But his grip was like steel, and she was helpless. Or would be if she had actually wanted to be free.

Watching his free hand glide over her breast, then stomach, and then her core, she noticed his eyes watching his hand on her body. It was erotic as hell.

If she had known a year ago that he would be this good in bed, she would have seduced him. Sure, she had thought about being in bed with him, but it had never been this good—and her imagination was very good.

Just a light touch of his fingers sliding over her core again made her back arch off the bed as she gasped. He played her body with careful strokes, and she let him. Her orgasm hit fast and hard, rolling through her and making her toes curl.

While her body was still convulsing, Kaine let go of her hands. She was spent and couldn't get her body to move, so she left them above her head. Still breathing heavily, she opened her eyes, only to catch a glimpse of his penis before he slammed it into her wet, hot core.

He slipped in easily and filled her to the hilt, then stopped, letting her adjust to him being there. "Are you okay?"

"Don't stop," she hissed as her hips started rocking of their own accord, searching for release again as if it had been weeks instead of moments since her last one.

Kaine was not moving, not matching her movement. Stopping, she looked up at him. He was looking at her, just looking down at her with a smile on his lips. Then he lowered himself to her and kissed her, crushing their lips together. She let in his searching tongue and met it. Finally able to move her hands, she ran them through his hair and held him to her, feasting on his mouth.

Pulling his lips from hers, he smiled down at her as he gripped her hips. After pulling out slowly, he plunged back, in making her gasp as her body met his rhythm. His tempo was fast, or maybe it was hers. Either way, they were both satisfied based on the noises each made as she met and matched his every thrust.

With her body still humming from the first orgasm, a second ripped through her, making her quiver and convulse. Within seconds, he plunged in deep and stiffened as his own orgasm overtook him.

Naked and sated, Harper couldn't move if she tried. Not that she was trying. Kaine's wet, sweating, sexy body was lying on top of hers. He, too, seemed unable to move. This was going to be the best month of her life.

"I guess we *are* compatible in bed." She giggled as he slid off her and onto the bed beside her.

"I was hoping the money wasn't what was making you wet." His finger traced her collar bone.

"Didn't even think about it," she admitted. And nor would she ever have to. Kaine showed the same determination in the bedroom as in the office. Only it was way less annoying in the bedroom.

"Good. Did you want to shower?" he asked.

"Nope, I never want to get up again. I plan to stay here forever." Not that she could, but a few more hours of sleep would be amazing.

"I'm going to since I have to work today." His words should have pissed her off, but not today. "Join me if you want."

"Nope, can't walk." She rolled over and hugged her pillow to her head.

His lips covered her back with kisses as he said, "Go to sleep, Nelle."

She groaned at the sound of her name. She should tell him to call her Harper, but she needed to keep this from becoming personal. This was just business. If she let him into her life, it became a relationship that could break her heart.

CHAPTER NINE

BY 5 P.M., he was ready to call it a day. Not that he was done with everything he had wanted to do today, but he wanted to go home. Leaving Nelle asleep in bed when he left this morning had been hard. Very hard.

Though he had been disappointed when she was asleep the night before, this morning had been mind-blowingly good. Better than he had ever expected it to be. When he had proposed the arrangement, he had thought that she would be accommodating in bed, letting him take charge. Instead, he had to fight for control of her, and at times, he had lost that control. She knew it and used it.

Now he was two hours from seeing her again, and he wondered what she was going to be like tonight. He had never suspected that her personality was different when she worked. He thought she was as type A as he was. For a year, she hadn't done or said anything that pointed to her ambition or take-charge attitude.

Bex walked into his office and tossed him a file. "Turner merger information you wanted."

"Thanks." He opened the file and looked through it.

Bex sat down across from him and folded her arms. "How was your evening?"

"Good, and yours?" He tried not to let her rattle him.

"Great. Arabella would like you to come over for supper on Friday. After seven. Bring a guest." She grinned at him. Her invitation meant his assistant had told his sister about Nelle, and the grin meant Bex probably exaggerated a bit.

Kaine didn't smile. "I can come, but Nelle's busy that night."

"Saturday then," Bex replied, not missing a beat.

"Nope. We have a previous engagement."

"Arabella will be calling you. You know you can't dodge her forever. She may just show up at your house, unannounced." Bex got up and walked out of the office. She had won that round.

Arabella was nothing if not persistent. Kaine wasn't worried that she would dislike Nelle; his sister liked everyone, and everyone liked her. It was for that reason her flower shop had been a success.

Though lately, she had let others run her shop since raising her son had taken precedence from the moment he was born. But Kaine was just happy she was happy. He knew he would have to call her and tell her about Nelle, but he didn't need to do it within days of hiring her.

By the time he had made it through the file, he was ready to call it a day and see how Nelle's day had gone. After saying goodbye to Christine, he headed home, happy to do so for the first time in years.

He was home by ten minutes to seven, but she wasn't there. Her Jeep wasn't in the drive. He knew she had an issue with promptness but had hoped she would get it under control.

After changing into jeans and a sweater, he headed down and saw her coming in the door. Her backpack was once again on her shoulder, and she smiled as she saw him and took her tennis shoes off at the door.

"Hi. You're home. I didn't think you would be yet." She pushed her blonde hair back behind her and slid off the backpack.

"I am. Did you have a good day?" Today she smelled of garlic and tomatoes. His stomach growled, and he wished they were having Italian tonight.

"Yes, very. I slept until after eight, then went home," she informed him. "I told the chef I was watching him, but I don't think he believed me."

He took the backpack from her. "What are you watching him for?"

"Messing up recipes. I'm going to have a problem with him." She opened the bag he was holding and pulled out a bag of chocolate chip cookies. "I made these today."

"Here?" He wondered how his chef would take that.

"No, at home. I even got them done before noon." She took her backpack back from him.

"That's good. It's good to hear you had a good day." He was left standing there, holding a bag of cookies.

"Didn't you? I mean, you were working, and you love to work." Her brown eyes looked at him closely.

"It was okay. I mean, I didn't get any baking done, but we both can't bring home cookies." He followed her as she headed to the kitchen, backpack once again slung over her shoulder.

"You're right. What did Philip make tonight? He said I should check the menu, as if he couldn't just tell me the words." She tossed her backpack on a stool.

"Steak Diane, one of my favorites," he informed her as she moved easily through his kitchen.

"And he remakes that for you? It isn't too dry?" She opened the oven and looked inside.

"No. I haven't had any issues with it before." He moved her aside, and with an oven mitt, pulled one of the plates from the oven and set it in front of her.

"Good for you. Willing to overlook bad cooking." She analyzed the meal on the warm plate.

"Has anyone told you that you're particular?" He pulled the other plate out.

"Hundreds of times." She didn't take any offense. "Picky, demanding, control freak. I'm fairly certain you've been told that a time or two yourself."

"Can't say I have." He watched her get silverware out of the drawer.

She stopped and looked at him. "Is that a joke? Did Mr. Hawthorn tell a joke?"

She cut into the steak and ate a tiny bite, really tiny, and made a face. She pushed the plate away from her, then pulled it back and slid it away again.

"You don't like it?" He nodded at the dish.

She pulled it back to her again. "Does it always taste this way?"

"I haven't tried it tonight yet." His plate was next to hers on the other side of her.

Quickly, she cut another sliver of beef and held it out for him to eat from her fork. Taking it, he chewed it carefully and nodded. "That's how it usually is."

Pushing the plate away from her once again, she turned to him all serious. "I don't want to tell you how to live your life, Kaine, but if you pay to have a personal chef, they should be here to serve you the meal every day. That's their job."

"My hours are unpredictable," he argued. He never knew when he came home in the evening.

"Don't have a chef then. Eat out every night; you can afford it. But if you're paying someone to make you food, make time in your life to eat it. Reheated meals aren't worth what you're paying for them."

"I don't like eating out." He folded his arms.

"Then stop working sixteen hours a day so your chef can feed you food at the moment it's supposed to be served. You pay too much for this."

"I have the money, Nelle, and I like the food. Are you going to eat with me tonight?"

Her brown eyes flashed with anger still. "No, I already ate."

"You knew that there was food here for you." He pointed to the plates on the counter.

She laughed as she grabbed him a glass of water and one for herself. "That is *not* food. It was spaghetti night tonight. Italian. I had to leave early, but I ate."

"I don't only eat French food." He took a bite of the semi-dry beef again, wishing it were Italian to match her smell. "Nice shirt."

Looking down at her shirt, she chuckled. The yellow shirt said "Yalling Stan" today. "It should say 'Yellow Stone.' I always wished she'd made a 'Yelling Stan' one. That would have been funny. I forgot your shirt. I have to make a note."

"Can I change it to one like this?"

"Nope, this one is one of a kind. I had to steal it from Mom. She usually has all the fun ones. She's sneaky and does everyone's laundry just to gather them back."

"Your mom does your laundry?"

"Not always. Just when she's in a mood. She's an organizing freak, and when she's emotional, she cleans. It's handy, actually." She chuckled.

"You live with her?"

"Yes, I do." Suddenly, her back was up. "I've lived on my own before, but I like it there."

"You go back there during the day?"

"You can't ask what I do, per the contract." She folded her arms. But it was obvious that she just goes home during the day. He didn't even know what was in the backpack she carried back and forth every day.

"You're right. We're going to a function on Saturday night. Do you need a dress?"

"Where at? What's it for?"

"The J, and it's a charity thing for the new library." He took another bite of the beef.

"Wow, I always wanted to see inside The J. Have you been before?" She sat on a stool beside him.

"Yes, a few times. Do you need a dress?" Most people didn't know about The J since it typically held events for the super-rich.

"No, that's okay. I'll borrow one of Mom's." She poked at a potato on his plate with her finger.

"I'll buy you a new one." He watched her frown at the potato in amusement. She was cute when she judged food that was offered to her.

"No need. I know which one I want. I'll just have to get it cleaned," she mussed and took his fork and ate a small bite of the potato, then gave the fork back to him.

"You and your mother wear the same size? Same style?" He made a mental note to make sure to get her a dress, just in case her mom's dress wasn't as nice as she needed.

"Sure, she's a size smaller and a bit taller than me, so everything's tighter and longer, but it's doable." She shrugged.

He would argue with her, but they did wear the same T-shirt. Also, the kind of dress she would need wasn't something that would be hanging in her mother's closet.

"I'll just have you get something new," he said again.

"I swear to you that it'll be perfect. If it isn't, I will eat one of these French things you eat." She shot him a grin.

"For a week," he countered.

"Fuck, a week," she agreed. He wondered if she doubted her plan now.

"Yup, no eating at home." He pointed to her with his fork. He could see she was coming up with a runaround.

"I would never. Did you find a replacement for me at work yet? I know I'm indispensable and all."

"Bex had someone there soon after you left." He didn't want to make her feel like Bex didn't like her and that she hadn't been appreciated when she was his personal assistant.

"I knew she would. She's had someone picked out for my job for months. But I showed her—I don't quit." She pounded the counter with her fist once for emphasis.

"Did she harass you to quit?" He needed to know. Bex was his right hand.

"No, but she doesn't like me. She made that perfectly clear."

"I'll talk to her." He didn't want that happening at his company; he wanted people to feel liked at work.

"Don't worry about it. I'm here and am not going back there," she assured him. "I'm going to take my bag upstairs, okay?"

She jumped off the stool and grabbed her bag from the seat next to her, not waiting for an answer.

Again, he wondered what she had done all day. Eaten with her family, obviously, but that was all she really said. Today she hadn't seemed the least bit tired; she was nothing but restless energy. It was a side of her that he had never seen at the office. He wondered if he would have been able to keep his hands off her if she had been outgoing and interesting at work. If she had what seemed like restless energy there, could he have stayed away?

Pushing his plate away half-eaten, he shut the lights off as he followed her upstairs to see if this morning had been a fluke, and she wasn't his dream come true in the bedroom. Once in the room, he found her slipping out of her jeans.

Her eyes met his as she straightened and tossed the pants on the floor near her feet. He wondered if she was testing him about keeping the house clean.

"Are you going to leave them there?" he asked as he pulled his sweater over his head and folded it.

"Yep. I'll wear them home tomorrow, so there's no need to put them away." She glanced at them and kicked them further into the wall with her foot.

Kaine put the sweater in a drawer as he said, "I would prefer that you put them somewhere other than the floor at night."

"That's where you and I differ. I prefer the lived-in look." Her eyes were locked on his as she pulled off her yellow T-shirt, revealing an equally yellow bra.

"I like things tidy." His eyes were on her breasts now, and her chest was heaving slightly. He was either getting on her nerves or turning her on.

Whichever it was, she did a half-grin and reached up to unclasp her bra. Pulling it off, she tossed it to him. He caught it and held it.

"Put that away." She grinned at him with her naked breasts taking all his attention.

This morning, he hadn't been able to see and appreciate the pale mounds, but now that they were on display, he was very happy with choosing her. He liked way more than her body, but her body was gorgeous.

"I don't know where it goes. It's yours."

"You were the last to touch it. It's yours now." She reached down and pulled off a sock and tossed it to him, but he didn't catch it. He didn't even try.

"That's not how it works," he pointed out as she threw another sock at him, hitting him in the head this time.

"You live by *my* rules, Kaine. If you touch it, it's yours." She laughed an evil laugh as she picked up her shirt from the bed, most likely to throw it at him.

Instantly, he dropped the bra and stalked over to her, grabbing her around the waist. His fingers gripped her soft, warm skin. "I've touched you, so that makes you mine."

Her eyes were instantly wide and then dark as she gasped with surprise. Before she could say a witty response, his lips claimed hers. He pulled her tighter to him, feeling her bare chest against his.

His breathing was ragged when he pulled his lips from hers, then lifted her off the ground to bring her nipples to his lips. To his delight, her legs wrapped around his waist.

Taking her other nipple in his mouth, he said huskily, "Your breasts are beautiful."

Her only response was to grab his head by his hair and drag his mouth back to hers. He knew he would have to fight for control again, but he was ready.

Her legs were wrapped so tight around him that he didn't have to hold her up, which meant his hands were free to wander over her body. She was only in yellow panties, and he wanted to touch every exposed inch of her—and the unexposed.

Her hands had left his hair and were now exploring his body as he suckled her breasts again.

"Bed now," she demanded as her sly fingers unbuttoned his pants.

"Not yet," he replied, moving to the other breast.

She pushed his lips from her breast. "Yes."

"No." He grabbed at her as she leaned away from him.

But she was too far away from him, and gravity pulled them both onto the bed. The little devil had gotten her way. Her grin of satisfaction was adorable.

CHAPTER TEN

SHE HAD FOUND her routine within a day: get up late and check on the help, and then head for home. But on Wednesday, she had the day off. So, after a small skirmish with Philip, then telling the two maids that she had been checking, and they were not cleaning everything properly, she headed out. It was her job to make sure they were doing what was needed at the house. It wasn't her fault that her standards were higher than they were used to.

She had decided to make a point of checking in with the help every day; if not, he was just paying her for sex, and that felt gross. Okay, the sex part felt very, very good, but the money part of it was gross. Kaine knew his way around the bedroom and her body—she had no complaints there.

Tonight, she wouldn't see him for the first time since this started. Waking up early with him hadn't been a chore, though she was happy she could sleep for a few more hours after he'd left. She felt it was goodbye sex, even if she was coming back the next day. She was sure she would miss the sex during her day off, but who wouldn't?

Pushing into her mom's house, she was happy to see Lucy up and working. Usually, she had to drag Lucy from her bed. Harper liked the change in her sister. She was taking her added responsibility seriously.

"You made it! I have the chicken marinating, and it should be ready at noon to start baking." Lucy was still in her pajamas but seemed happy to be up.

"What do you want me to do?" She went to the sink to wash her hands.

Yesterday they had hired a contractor for the kitchen remodel, and he would start sometime today. Harper still didn't know where they were going to cook when he was in the middle of it, but tomorrow, she was going to look for a spot to rent for a month. Everything was going according to plan.

"Peel potatoes. I'm cutting carrots."

"Okay," Harper said, even if she wanted to do the cutting and have Lucy peel. She was trying to let go. Who knew it was going to be so hard? But for Lucy, she would do it. "Anyone else home today?"

"Ag and Buzz. I think Maby had a class this morning. Or she stayed at Cliff's. She probably stayed with Cliff." Mabel taught literature at the local college, and nobody could keep her schedule straight. And now, she had half moved in with her fiancé.

"How are Maby and Cliff doing? Still on?" she asked. It had only been a few days, but for Harper, those two days had been highly eventful.

"Hot and heavy. This is it for Maby." Lucy grinned.

"How are you with them together? Cliff was yours first," Harper asked tentatively. She had never heard that Lucy and Cliff were more than friends, that either had those types of feelings for the other. But the sisters were identical twins.

From the moment Harper realized something was up between Mabel and Lucy's best friend, she worried about Lucy reacting badly to the news. And she had for a day, and then she was over it, and all for her sister's relationship. But could she really be all for her sister's love life?

Harper hadn't missed that her sister had instantly bounced back into bed with her ex the night Mabel and Cliff got together—an ex that was seeing someone else and was already cheating on her with another woman. Lucy meant nothing to him, but Lucy couldn't seem to let him go.

"I love Cliff, and I love that he's in love with Maby. They're cute together." Lucy cut more carrots.

Looking over at her, Harper wondered how alike or different Lucy thought she looked from Mabel They were hard to tell apart even now. Both preferred the same hairstyle and clothing most of the time. Harper had flubbed their names in the last year, but neither thought they looked alike.

"They are. Did you know who he was?" Harper asked. It had recently come out that he was the son of one of the old money families in town, something that he had only admitted after he had proposed to Mabel, though Mabel had known for a while.

"Nope, but I never cared. As long as I didn't have to buy him drinks when we went out. I don't have that kind of money, anyway," Lucy said.

"We will one day, sister. We're taking this business to the top." Harper tossed a few potato peelings at her little sister.

"Dork," Lucy replied, tossing a few carrots her way. "How is your boss going to survive you being gone for a day?"

"He was surviving before I came." She tried not to blush at her poor choice of words.

"I'm going to let that one go. Too easy, just like you." Lucy tossed another handful of carrots at her.

"Bitch." She tossed more peelings at her, mostly hit their mark this time. That made Lucy laugh.

By the time the small food fight was over, Harper had been reduced to actually throwing potatoes at her sister, and there were no longer any carrots cut. The floor was covered in wet, slippery vegetables, and they were behind schedule.

When she finally climbed into her old bed at midnight, she was exhausted. She missed Kaine. It had been three days, and she was already missing him. What was going to happen after thirty?

CHAPTER ELEVEN

IT WASN'T that Kaine didn't believe Nelle's mom wasn't a great dresser; he just didn't think it would be appropriate on a thirty-year-old. On Wednesday morning, he had his personal shopper pick up a dress for her to wear to the event that night. Her mom had to be close to fifty, if not older. He didn't want to show up with Nelle wearing what a fifty-year-old would wear.

Nelle had been off since Friday morning. That day, he had taken the opportunity to work a few extra hours on Friday since he had no one to come home to. He didn't want to admit it, but he was enjoying being home almost as soon as she was. He liked spending time with her.

Still, she never said what she did during her day, and he had refrained from asking. Not that he was complaining about what she did when she was away from him, because when she was with him, she was focused on him. She was the perfect mistress. The pattern had been set. She came home and watched him eat, then complained about the food she wasn't even eating because she had always already eaten by then. They would talk for a while, and then they would go to bed. Though she wasn't as exhausted as she was before, she didn't complain about early nights. Usually, it was quite the opposite.

In case the borrowed dress wasn't to his liking, the black dress he had purchased for her was in the closet in the spare bedroom.He waited for her in the rarely used living room. He himself was rarely home enough to just sit in there.

At a little after 5 p.m., she wordlessly rushed into the house in her usual jeans and T-shirt. Kaine only caught a glimpse of her as she ran up the stairs, only seeing that her makeup was done and that her blonde hair was piled on her head. A bag hung over her shoulder.

Ten minutes later, she walked down the stairs in black heels and a red dress with a slit up the side almost to her panty line. His eyes traveled north across the shimmery red fabric that hugged her curves and made her breasts overflow the cups a little more than they should.

She must have seen where his eyes were because she tried to stuff them more into the dress. "I know, Luce said it looked great, but I think they're trying to choke me."

"You look stunning." His eyes raked her body again, memorizing the vision. He suddenly wished he hadn't promised to be there that night.

"I couldn't find Mom's red 'fuck me' heels. I think she wore them to work. That whore."

"Did she work today? And did you just call her a whore?" He tried to hide his shock at her description of her own mom, but if she looked anywhere as good as her daughter in the red dress, any man would be lucky to have the woman.

"No, not today, but she didn't come home after work on Friday. She goes to her boyfriend's house a lot. He really likes her 'fuck me' heels." She shrugged.

"The black ones are very nice. I can't believe I questioned your mom's taste in clothes." He couldn't control his smile as he took her hand, all earlier doubt gone.

She grinned as she took the last step to the main floor. "Harry's."

"What?"

"Her boyfriend. He dresses her for events. Mom would never let her boobs hang out, but Harry likes them."

"He has good taste."

"Of course, Kaine. He's marrying Sera."

"You're right. Did I tell you that you're gorgeous yet?"

"Yes, you might have said it once. You clean up pretty nicely your-self, though your ass looks way better in jeans." She grabbed it and squeezed as he led her to the garage. They were already behind sched-ule, and all he could think about was not going to this event he already didn't want to go to.

Opening the door to the Porsche, he wondered if she would rather drive the Lincoln SUV, but based on her smile, she was okay with his choice.

They backed out of the garage, and he saw she was driving a blue Jeep today. So far, there had been four different colors, but they were all the exact same year and style.

"Why all the Jeeps?" he asked as she looked over the sports car and touched the dash and radio controls.

"Mom and Agatha can fix them. No garage bills."

"The owner of this dress fixes your car?"

"Sure. Her dad was a mechanic or something like that. She never talks about it much. And she never wears a dress when she's working on them." She fell silent as she scanned through the radio stations.

He watched her concentrate on the radio and said, "Your tattoo is gone."

"Lucy put enough cover-up on it to make it go away for a while. When she put my hair up, she said she would make it go away. Thank god. I rarely wear it up because of it." She seemed to find a station she liked and leaned back in the seat, but then she sat forward again and changed the channel.

"You regret getting it?" He lightly touched the vanished tattoo.

"Yes, stupid and fifteen."

"Your mom agreed to it?"

"Sera? Never. Dad signed for it. He would sign anything if you said it was for school. Bonus was he never read anything that he signed. Sera said it was a learning opportunity, and I learned not to get another one."

"A harp?"

Her phone buzzed in her hand, and she looked at it, reading the screen. Grinning, she said, "Lucy will be at The J in the back parking lot with the shoes. Mom came home."

"Is your house near The J?"

"Yes, about a mile. In the Allering Addition."

"All those old houses?"

"Yup, Judith loved old, big houses. Not that I'm complaining. I love the house and can't see being raised anywhere else." She pointed to a Jeep in the back of the lot.

"Judith?" he asked as he pulled to a stop by the brunette Nelle had been with the night at the bar. That night, he hadn't noticed that they looked alike, but tonight he did.

"My real mom." She hopped out of the car and almost ran around the front of the car.

If Judith was her mom, who was Sera? Stepmom? She mentioned a lot of names, so her family must be large, though she rarely took the time to explain who any of them were.

Kaine watched her step out of the black shoes and slip on the red ones as she held on to her sister's arm for balance. She and the brunette talked the entire time. Kaine couldn't hear what she was saying, but it was mostly about either him or the car because she pointed with her free arm.

As he waited, he could tell they were related. Even though their hair was different shades, they had the same mannerisms and build. They both laughed at something, and Nelle pushed her sister a bit harder than was needed, and her sister stumbled a little. But she didn't stop laughing.

Nelle walked back around the car, flipping her sister off as she did. Kaine rolled down his window to hear the barbs that were going between the sisters.

"May your tits fall out of that dress over the dry chicken, Harps!" Lucy yelled.

"May your next hook-up have a tiny dick, Luce."

"I'm going to tell mom you're stealing her clothes."

"I'm going to tell mom you're getting married."

"What?!" Lucy said and started to run around the car at her sister. Nelle slid into the car and slammed the door closed before her sister was past the front of the car.

Kaine looked over at Nelle. "Is she getting married?"

"No, but Mom would be so excited, and then Lucy would have to tell her she's not. Nobody likes to make Mom sad or mad." She waved at her sister, who was standing outside her door.

"You just got into a fight with your sister in the parking lot?"

"No, we had words. It's only a fight when you touch," she replied, looking down at her dress to make sure her boobs were still inside it, and then adjusted them. His dick took notice.

"Is she older or younger than you?" He pulled his eyes from her chest.

"Younger, but a brat still. I am mature and responsible." She turned to see if the sister was chasing the car. She was not.

"I can see that. The picture of maturity." He pulled up to the door and stopped for the valet.

Once around the car, he opened the door for her, and his mouth went dry again. A week before, he had thought she was plain. Today she took his breath away. He knew she would be the most beautiful woman in the room, and she was going home with him at the end of the night.

"Smiles, Kaine. Look happy to be here. Everyone loves you," she whispered as the doors opened, and they walked into the party already in full swing.

Within an hour, they had made their way around the entire room, and Kaine was ready to leave. No way was he staying through the meal with her in that dress. Not that she was going to eat anything anyway. She had taken four appetizers and hadn't eaten one, just tossed them after looking at them.

"Kaine, it's nice to see you tonight. I don't believe I've met your date before." Conrad Williams stopped him in his tracks. Conrad was on the board to raise money for the library and had worked with Kaine a few years before on a project.

"Hello, Conrad." He faked a smile; he wanted out of there. "This is

Nelle Lovely. Nelle, this is Conrad Williams."

Conrad took her hand as she smiled, something she had been doing since the moment they walked into the room. Not once had it broken. Releasing his hand, she smiled brighter, as if it was possible. "Hello, Mr. Williams."

"Miss Lovely, you look stunning tonight." His eyes swept her body with most of his concentration on her breasts, but she didn't react to it.

"A girl just likes a chance to dress up. Don't you think, Kaine?" She turned to him, focusing Conrad's attention back on him. It was so quick, he barely noticed how well she did it.

"That's all these things are," Kaine agreed.

"But this one is an important one. Raising money for the library." Conrad frowned, but then his eyes caught someone more interesting, and he headed in that person's direction without another word.

"Did you want to sit for a while?" He couldn't resist whispering it in her ear.

"Yes, my feet are killing me. Nobody warned me that 'fuck me' heels hurt." She ran her hand down the front of his tux jacket.

"This way." He led them to a table and pulled out her chair. Sitting next to her, he said, "Are you having fun?"

"Fun is maybe strong, but it's interesting. Are we staying for the meal?"

"Up to you. It's probably chicken." He touched her leg because he needed to.

"No, it's grilled beef tenderloin with horseradish sauce, red baby potatoes, and a chocolate cake for dessert."

"How do you know?" he asked in surprise. He hadn't heard anyone say anything about the meal.

"I asked a waiter. They always know. The beef will be tough, though. You can't do it well with this many people." She wrinkled her nose as she always did when talking about food.

"What would you rather have?" Leaning back in his chair, he wondered if he would ever actually see her eat. He doubted it.

"Pizza. Would you eat pizza?" she asked.

"Italian? I don't know." He would eat anything with her.

"Excuse me, Mr. Hawthorn. Is that chair taken?" A redhead in a black cocktail dress and a sassy smile asked, pointing at the chair beside him. The one his back was currently to.

Looking at the chair in question, he said, "No, go ahead and take it."

The redhead moved to the chair, and he turned back to Nelle until the redhead slid her chair right between them. "Thank you. I'm Bea Bradford with the Times, and I have a few questions for you if you don't mind."

Sitting up straight, he looked at her gray eyes and wondered who would be interested in him. He wasn't rich enough in this town for people to care, but this woman seemed to. In fact, she seemed overly interested in him for some reason.

He sat up straight. "Sure. What do you want to know?"

"Bea, I'm sure that Mr. Hawthorn is not who your readers want to read about," Nelle interjected, her eyes on the redhead also.

"And you are?" The redhead turned to her with interest, pen in hand.

"I assume your paper really wants a story on Clifton Scott or Andrew Vincent or even Eric Andrews." Nelle pointed to the men in question. It was odd to Kaine that she knew who they were. He hadn't introduced her to any of them, and he barely knew them himself. He may be rich, but not that rich.

"I have others working on that angle." The redhead looked back at him. "How much are you planning on sponsoring for the new library?"

"I haven't put a number on it yet," he said and watched as she didn't write it down.

"I don't think reporters are even allowed in here, Bea Bradford." Nelle looked around the room again as if she could tell no other reporters were there.

She turned to him again. "I'm here as a date, not a reporter. What does your company do, exactly?"

"I don't know if I want my name in the paper." He folded his arms, tired of this line of questioning.

"Everyone wants their name in the paper; their fifteen minutes of fame," she declared with a grin.

"I'll have to ask you to leave us alone before I call security," he told her, and her grin died as she quickly glanced at Nelle.

"Well, I have never. I have bigger fish to talk to than you, Mr. Hawthorn." She got up and walked away in a huff.

Turning back to his date, he saw Nelle was watching the redhead walk away also. "I don't think the bigger fish are talking either."

"Well, I'm not talking to her," he stated. She had just done a one-eighty on the woman the instant she was gone, as if she regretted treating her like she had.

"Didn't say you should." She turned back to him and glanced at the kitchen as a waiter came out. "What were we talking about?"

"Leaving this place and getting a pizza," he reminded her, and she grinned.

"What kind do you like?"

"Sausage, just that."

"I can handle that." She looked around the room, and her eyes stopped on the redhead before coming back to him.

"You're not going to wrinkle your nose at it and declare it unfit for consumption?" He took her hand, trying to ignore her interest in the reporter. A lot of people were interested in the public knowing about them, but not him.

"I don't do that. Ever." She turned to him and said with a half-grin.

"No, you don't. Your right," he agreed with a grin of his own.

"I'm always right. You will soon learn that about me." Her eyes went to the kitchen.

"We should leave soon if we don't want to get stuck with the meal," he pointed out. "But I have to go to the men's room before we leave."

"Go ahead. I'll wait here for you." She let go of his hand.

Getting up, he admired her breasts again and quickly headed to the men's room so that they could leave. He wanted her back at his house and wished they had never left.

CHAPTER TWELVE

"Your date ditch you?" Bea Bradford asked, sitting down next to Harper on the other side of where she had been before. Bea, whose actual name was Beatrix Potter Lovely, used their dad's name Bradford when she reported. She said Bea Lovely just didn't cut it on a byline for a murder or fatal accident.

"Went to the men's room. He'll be back." She looked at her baby sister, who always went by Buzz with the family, and wondered why the perky, interesting redhead was having such a hard time with reporting. But Buzz had a hard time with any job.

"Maybe he already left. Reporters scared him off." Buzz grinned at her joke.

"Nope, he's coming back."

"That's because no man would leave those tits, Harps." Buzz looked at them.

"I know. A pushup bra has nothing on this dress. I don't remember Mom looking so chesty in it." She tried to tuck her boobs further into the dress.

"She isn't as chesty as you. How's your date? He's cute." Buzz grinned at her sister. It seemed the little skirmish wasn't enough for Buzz to stop liking Kaine.

"He's my boss, so he doesn't get to touch anything." She looked at her chest as she lied. No way was he not touching her tonight, and she was looking forward to it. So was he, based on the way his eyes had been eating her up all night. "These are all mine."

"That's not what his eyes were saying, Harps. They were saying 'all mine,' also. Boss or not, he looks like he's going to touch. A lot." Buzz wrinkled up her nose at the thought.

"He can appreciate me," she admitted, as Buzz rolled her eyes at her statement. "Nobody will talk to you?"

"No, they see me as a novice reporter not worth their time." Buzz blew a curl from her face.

"Which you are. It hasn't even been a year. Last year, you were working at a museum," Harper reminded her.

"I know, but it feels like a long time ago. A very long time ago." Buzz leaned back in her chair, and they both watched the kitchen door as waiters went in and out. "Don't you have a gorgeous date to watch instead of analyzing your competition?"

"Nope, he's my boss. Von Shild keeps getting The J. Why?" she said out loud. She had been thinking about it all night.

"Because everyone knows him as the guy who caters at The J," Buzz reminded her.

"I want to cater here. And not just for a wedding party every now and again. I want to be here for every party." Harper looked at the door and saw another waiter come out happily. She knew she would be happy here.

"Don't we have lofty dreams?" Buzz giggled a little.

"Do I have to call security, Ms. Bradford?" Kaine looked down at the redhead, who instantly straightened up and looked at him. Harper was sure she didn't miss the anger in his face.

"Nope, just leaving." Buzz got up.

"It's okay, Kaine. We were just having a little chat." Harper looked up at his angry face.

"About what?" he demanded.

"About you, mostly," Buzz replied in true Buzz fashion. But her words didn't cause the laugh Harper was sure Buzz was trying to get from the man.

"I don't want to see my name in the newspaper in the morning, Ms. Bradford. Do you understand?" Kaine said.

Getting up, Harper replied, "Bea will not put anything in the paper about you. Isn't that right, Beatrix?"

"I can assure you, Mr. Hawthorn, nothing about you will get in the paper." Buzz held up her hand as if swearing on a bible.

"What were you chatting about?" Kaine asked again, as if they had been caught doing something that they weren't allowed to do.

"None of your fucking business!" Buzz barked at Kaine. Then she turned to Harper and said, "I would fucking quit if I were you. Don't let him treat you that way. What a fucking ass."

Watching Buzz walk away, Harper was completely on her side—he was being an ass to both of them, not just Buzz. They could talk all they wanted to. In fact, they talked almost every fucking day. He had no control over her life. She may work for him, but she didn't deserve to be treated that way.

"What a bitch," Kaine stated, also watching her.

"She was right. You are an ass." She plopped down in her chair, still facing the kitchen door.

"I thought we were leaving?"

"No, thank you. I'll catch a ride home tonight. Nobody talks to me like that—*nobody*." She stared again at the door to the kitchen.

"I'll take you to my place. You have a contract, Nelle," he hissed in her ear.

He was right, which only added to her anger. Not a week before, she had signed up for anything, and that meant this. Even if she suddenly questioned whether she could do this.

"Take me to your place then!" she hissed right back at him.

Neither spoke until they were back at his place; the only noise was the purr of the motor. Inside the tiny car, the anger was still palpable. Once back and inside the house, she went to his bedroom and grabbed her backpack off the bed. After she grabbed the hanger and bag that the dress had been in, she turned to leave, but he was in the doorway.

Trying to push past him with her stuff, she growled when he pinned her to the wall.

"Where are you going?" he demanded angrily.

"Home. I will not be treated like this, Kaine Hawthorn. Nowhere in the contract does it say you can treat me like shit." she yelled as she tried to push his body away from hers. She couldn't do this anymore.

"What the fuck? I come back, and you're chatting with a reporter, and neither one of you would say what you were talking about. How was I supposed to take that?" He pried the hanger from her hand and threw it down the hallway.

"What do you think we were talking about? Nobody fucking cares about you. I have never seen your name in the paper." She pushed at his chest with all her might.

"She seemed interested in who I was," he pointed out.

Laughing harshly at him, she said, "Not you, you pig-headed oaf. She had no interest in talking to you at all. She wanted to talk to me."

"And why would she do that?" His tone pissed her off even more.

"So, I'm nothing? Oh, yeah, I forgot. I'm just someone for you to fuck when you want. Not an actual person who might be interesting, and who people might just want to talk to." She pushed even harder against his chest.

"That is not how I see you, Nelle. I know you're interesting, but some reporter doesn't care about that. They're only in it for the story. They'll run over anyone who gets in the way!" he yelled.

"Not her. You don't know her."

"I saw enough of her to know she was rude and brash. And a fucking bitch," he hissed

At his words, though her hands were pinned to her side, she kneed him in the balls. Immediately, he dropped her arms to hold his crushed balls. Hard.

"Don't you *ever* call my sister a bitch. She's just doing her fucking job, just like me. Except she doesn't have to fuck an asshole at her job!" she yelled and walked past him, grabbing the hanger from the hallway.

Down the hallway and halfway down the stairs, her ankle gave out in the red heels, and she fell the rest of the way down, landing on the hardwood floor at the bottom. Laying there assessing the damage, she watched as Kaine ran down the dangerous steps towards her.

"Nelle? Are you okay? Talk to me." He sat on his knees before her.

"I might be okay. Just a little dazed," she admitted, putting a hand on her head.

"How far did you fall down?"

"Around half. I don't know. I have to leave." She sat up and cringed at the movement. Though nothing was broken, a bunch was hurting.

"Don't leave. Why didn't you tell me she was your sister?" His eyebrows were drawn in concern.

"Professional lines. She was working, and I was a guest. I didn't want to interfere with her job." She rubbed her elbow.

"And that means you don't talk to her? Say hi?" He ran his hands over her arms and legs, checking for damage.

"She *was* being a bitch. She only talked to you to get at me, but we talked when you were gone. I haven't seen her much this week," she replied, trying to get up.

"Just say hi next time. Maybe even introduce me." He lifted her from the ground and carried her up the stairs.

"She was working," she reminded him. He had never worked in the service industry, so he didn't understand, but it was all she knew.

"Then just whisper in my ear, 'the redhead is my sister. The one who looks nothing like me, that one.'" He took her down the hallway to his bedroom, and she didn't fight it.

"She looks like me. Just shorter, with red hair and different color eyes." She and Buzz had the same personality, but maybe not anything else.

"She does, now that I look back on it." Setting her on the bed, he pulled the backpack from her shoulder. "What's her real name?"

"Beatrix Lovely, Bea Lovely." She flopped back onto the bed. "She didn't want to use Lovely while reporting, so she uses Bradford. Dad's name."

Harper watched him slide out of his jacket and lay it on the dresser, then added the tie to the pile. Then he walked to the bed while kicking off his shoes.

"What does Bradford Lovely do?" He picked up her leg, ran his hand down it, and slid her shoe off.

"English professor, somewhere down south or east? Maybe still in South America. I don't actually know." She tried not to giggle as his lips ran over her toes.

"You don't communicate with him?" He slid his hand down her other leg.

"No, I haven't seen him since I was fifteen." Her shoe slipped off and fell to the floor.

"Half your life?" He started to pull the pins that held her hair up as their eyes met and held.

"I guess. I don't think about him anymore." She felt him run his hands through her hair as it tumbled down her back.

"My father was an ass also. I haven't seen him in close to a dozen years." He placed light kisses across her forehead with his fingers still tangled in her hair.

"You never talk about your family." She couldn't think of a time he had said anything about them. Maybe they didn't exist.

"You do all the time, but don't." He slid down the zipper on the back of her dress.

"They're a big part of my life." She shrugged, and her boobs popped out of the dress, finally escaping tight confinement.

His fingers traced the red line the bust line had made from back to front. "I have a younger sister who lives about a mile from here, and I see her a few times a month. She is married with a son and a baby on the way."

"You have me beat. Nobody in my family has kids." His hands caressed her as he slid her dress down her body and tossed it to the floor, leaving her in her red panties and nothing else.

"Condoms are an amazing invention," he reminded her, which made her laugh.

"That they are. The pill is pretty good also."

Harper watched as Kaine unbuttoned his pressed white shirt. She loved his body and couldn't believe it took her an entire year to notice it. Maybe because he was super annoying when he worked.

"You're very open about sex." He worked with the cuffs, leaving the shirt gaped in the front.

"I live in a house full of women who have sex. It's discussed a bit. Bea is the youngest, and she's twenty-five now." Her eyes were on his chest as he pulled the shirt from his shoulders.

"And you bring men home? To a house full of women?" His eyebrows raised.

"Yes, a shut door means stay out. Nobody cares." His dark eyes raked her naked body as he stood holding the shirt.

"I'm glad I have my own place. No running into your mom the morning after." Taking the shirt, he draped it over her shoulders and helped her get her arms in it. His touch was soft and delicate.

"That's what Mom's boyfriend says." She watched as he buttoned the shirt up for her.

"Smart man." He took her hand and pulled her off the bed. "I owe you a pizza that you promised you would eat."

"You're right; I did," she said, letting him lead her downstairs to the living room. In the week she had lived there, she hadn't spent much if any time in the rooms. If she had time to sit, she had time to go home.

"How is your body after the fall?" he asked, running a hand up her arms and over her shoulders.

"Okay, for now. I might be stiff tomorrow, though." Pushing his hands away, she sat down on the couch and curled her feet under her.

In his tux pants and no shirt, he called a gourmet pizza place that Harper hadn't eaten at before. For someone who just wanted sex from her, he was treating her nicely. She had to keep in mind that this was just sex, nothing more. No matter how he acted or treated her, she was nothing to him.

"Pizza will be here in forty-five minutes." He sat down across from her in a chair.

"Tell me about your sister," she pressed. She wanted to know more about him, not that she should.

"Arabella? Married for three years now. She used to work at the office for years, then she quit and started her own flower shop. She's the opposite of me; she got all the personality. Everyone loves her."

"My mom is just like that, too. The rest of us have learned to mimic her when needed. It really comes in handy." She couldn't say how many catering jobs had been gotten and saved by channeling Sera Lovely.

"Did you ever use it on me?"

"Absolutely. You can be pretty crabby in the morning."

"*Me*? You're a bear at four in the morning."

"Because nobody should have to work at that time. Offices work from eight to five, always.

"Eight hours aren't enough for me."

"You need to delegate more. You're a control freak. I was never late, and you constantly said I was," she reminded him.

"You had late person tendencies." He tapped her nose.

"Hey! I am an on-time person." She frowned at him.

"Punctual?" he raised an eyebrow as he asked.

"If you want to put a long word on it, smarty pants." She couldn't not laugh at his expression.

"Why did you move back from France?"

"A man. I lived with a man for most of my time there, and it kind of imploded, so I came home. I think it imploded because I secretly wanted to come back. I was missing the girls, and he was never going to move here." She hated a man being her reason that she did anything.

"Do you miss it? Besides the food?"

Settling more into the couch, she admitted, "Not really. It's been eight years, and I haven't thought about going back yet. Maybe one day, but not yet."

"You were young when you were there."

"Yep, just out of high school. It was a stupid time to go. Sera had to buy me tickets home for everyone's graduation. That was money she didn't have either. Of course, I didn't," she said. "Did you do anything foolish when you were young?"

"Not really. I went to college for four years. Got married the summer after. Then I started working for my father-in-law until I started my own business."

"Married? What happened to her?" Harper hadn't seen any evidence of a wife.

"She is now Mrs. James Horn. Apparently, I worked too much for her taste."

"You do. I would say the same thing. Delegate." The doorbell rang, and Kaine got up and soon brought back a white box that smelled of heaven.

"Shall we go to the dining room or kitchen?" he asked with box in hand.

"Neither. Right here." She tapped the couch, and he eyed it skeptically. "Come on, live a little."

Taking the box from him, she gave him the "I know best" look. He went and got drinks and napkins, and she opened the box and looked inside.

"No wrinkling your nose. You chose it." He tapped her on the nose as he walked by her.

"I do not wrinkle my nose! I'm a foodie, not a snob." She handed him a piece of pizza but took off a sausage and ate it.

"You *are* a food snob; there's no getting around it. This might be the first thing I have ever seen you eat." He took a bite of the pizza and moved the box from between them to the coffee table in front of them.

Laughing, she said, "I eat all the time, but French food does nothing for me. Now, this is good."

"You should have gone to Italy."

"I should have gone to New York—better pizza there. And closer." She finished her first piece and took another.

"So, your favorite is Italian? Should I get an Italian chef for the rest of the month?"

"No, just get a normal chef who can make anything. Variety is the spice of life, Kaine." She tossed the pizza slice back into the box.

Swinging a leg over him, she straddled him and took his pizza and tossed it into the box also. Without a word, she kissed him. He tasted of tomato sauce and sausage. He didn't resist, just slid his hands up her body under her shirt to cup her bare breasts.

Arching her back to him, she slowly unbuttoned his shirt, revealing his hands on her breasts below.

His lips grazed her chin as he whispered, "Are you sure?"

"Yes," was her response as she pulled the shirt off and tossed it on the floor.

"You were gorgeous in that dress, but even better right now." His blue eyes looked over her body, making her shake in anticipation.

Whether they got along or not outside the bedroom didn't matter. In it, they were perfect together. The sex was amazing every time.

CHAPTER THIRTEEN

It had been over twenty-four hours since Kaine had seen Nelle, and he hated to admit that he missed her. She had taken Tuesday off as well, but he had worked late and went in early, so he didn't miss her as much as Friday night into Saturday.

Saturday morning, he had driven to see his sister. It was something he hadn't done since he started his agreement with Nelle, which Arabella had known about since day one, thanks to Bex.

While sitting on the couch listening to Eddie chatter about his latest toy, he felt his sister judging him. Judging him harshly.

"Where is Bex this morning?" He had noticed she was missing when he arrived.

Her being gone was unusual. When not working, the couple was usually together, enjoying each other's company more than anyone else's. Their little family was the most important thing to both of them.

"Gym. She'll be back soon." Arabella leaned back in the chair. But her eyes remained on him, her blue eyes judging him. "How is your friend?"

There was no doubt that Bex had filled her in on the entire thing. At this point, Arabella probably knew more than Kaine did about the situation. Bex liked to exaggerate at times, and this would be one of those times.

"Good. She's off today." He looked at the toy his nephew handed him, an excuse not to look at his sister.

"I didn't know they got time off," Arabella commented.

"Really, she takes care of my house—that's all. She takes time off every day and gets two days off a week. Her choice of days," Kaine replied.

"Becca doesn't like her," Arabella stated, as if Kaine didn't already know that.

"Bex has her own opinion, but I happen to like the arrangement," Kaine said as Eddie scampered off.

Arabella looked at him closely. They looked a lot alike, with blond hair and blue eyes. Arabella was five years younger than him, and they only had each other since their parents had decided children weren't worth the hassle as adults. Adults had their own opinions about their lives, and their parents didn't seem to like any of those opinions.

"Tell me about her."

"She's blonde with brown eyes. She's tall and slim." He listed what Bex would have already told her. "She's also a food snob—a big food snob. I think every day she has off, she goes to her mom's house to spend time with her sisters and mom. When she was younger, she lived in France."

"How old is she? Becca said she was young." It seemed Bex hadn't painted a great picture for her wife.

"Thirty, so not young, really. Acts like it a lot, though. She still lives at home with her mom, who does her laundry."

"What is she going to do when this is done? Work for you still somewhere?"

"I don't know; we didn't talk about after. I'm hoping she stays where she is." He didn't want to talk about this with his little sister.

"Sex must be good then." Arabella couldn't stop smirking as she said it.

"Really, Arabella?"

"Hey, are you or are you not paying for sex, Kaine. It's an important aspect of it."

"She is not just there for sex," he argued.

"You like her then?" Arabella sat up and grinned at him. "Like, really like her?"

"I don't like her in that way; she's just fun to be around," he argued as the back door opened, and Eddie ran to see who it was.

"Because you like her. Are you falling for her?" Arabella demanded with a grin.

"No, I am not."

"I saw Kaine's car. Is he still here, or did he sneak out?" his assistant asked as she walked into the sunroom.

The suit she usually wore had been replaced by sweatpants and an oversized T-shirt, an outfit Kaine was now used to seeing her in. It was her "at home with the family" outfit.

"Kaine's falling for his hired woman." His sister took her wife's hands in hers.

When they had first gotten together, he had worried that the attraction would be short-lived and leave one or both shattered. If that happened, he would lose his right-hand woman, because he couldn't lose his sister.

They were both miserable after they'd broken up, and he couldn't stand it anymore, so he gently pushed them back together. He did that, and how did they reward him? Gang up on him about Nelle.

"He's had the hots for her for a year now. I can't see him not getting attached." Bex sat on the edge of Arabella's chair, slipping her arm around the other woman. No matter how Kaine felt about their relationship, they were still in love after almost three years.

"I am not 'attached,'" he said with finger quotes.

"He isn't working as much as he used to. Always home at seven now, and he hasn't been in at four since she started," Bex replied with a laugh.

"It has nothing to do with her," Kaine grumbled.

"This week, I called her Nelle with the 'E' at the end, and he almost flipped. 'It's just *Nelle*, no E sound at the end.'" Bex mocked his voice.

"It's her name," Kaine grumbled again.

"I want to meet her. If Kaine is in love, I need to see her," Arabella insisted.

"Not in love," He argued as the two exchanged a look, a look he didn't like. "I have to go."

Getting up, he hugged his nephew, and the women followed him to the door. Arabella hugged him and said, "I want you to be in love, Kaine."

"I'm not in love with her." He shook his head. This was a non-emotional relationship; that's what he loved, not her.

Now it was close to six, and he had been home for hours with nothing to do. Walking up to his bedroom, it still took him by surprise she had changed the bedding. The bedspread was a solid bright yellow, and she had removed all the heavy drapes, making the room lighter and airier.

When he asked her why she had done it, she had just said the other "wasn't him." At the time, he wondered if yellow was him but really, he'd known it was her preference.

As far as making sure the house was clean and his meals were made, she was a success. She hadn't made many changes, but some were long overdue.

Most of the week, she had been staying more at his house. Since Monday, she had been home when he got home. Usually, she was puttering around the house or in the kitchen. She must have told Philip who was in charge because this week, her cookies were in a jar on the counter.

Back downstairs, he was wondering how to spend the next hour before she came home when the front door burst open, and she hurried in. Her backpack was on her shoulder, and her arms were laden with small plastic containers.

Her energy made him smile, and he hurried over and grabbed the plastic containers from her. With a jaunty grin, she said thanks and left again.

Kaine hurried and put the containers in the fridge and went back to see what else she was bringing today. Never had she made two trips into his house with stuff. Usually, it was barely one.

By the time he was back at the door, she was already coming through it again, this time with a laptop and cord. Taking it from her, he saw that her orange shirt today said "Pancilvene" in bold gold letters.

"Pennsylvania?" He nodded at it. He loved guessing what they meant. She had been right; they were more fun than they first seemed.

"I think so. I love that the colors don't match." She grinned at him, and he noticed that her left eye was bluish purple.

She tilted her head at him, but it was still there. She had a black eye after her day off. What the hell could have happened to cause her to get a black eye?

"They're brown. I know they sometimes look blue, but they're are brown," she said, looking into his eyes.

"You have a black eye, Nelle." His teeth set as he stated the obvious.

She laughed, "I forgot. Happened yesterday."

"How? Did a man do this to you? Don't lie to me, Nelle." He was pissed. She was seeing someone else, and that someone was abusive. This wasn't the first bruise he had seen on her in the last two weeks. She usually laughed them off as accidents, but a black eye was different.

Pulling her head from his hands, she said, "What do you think happened, Kaine?"

"Have you been seeing someone else?"

"Oh, you mean the guy I see two days a week that's all too happy that I'm fucking you? But for some reason, he punched me in the eye a week later?" She questioned him as she took the computer back and headed to the kitchen.

"Something like that." He hated that he even had to ask and hated how it made him feel powerless and unable to protect her.

Setting the computer on the counter, she turned on him. "Let's see. Friday morning, I was teasing Agatha about losing another job and how she was going to be unemployable soon. She started chasing me through the house, and I fell onto the couch but rolled off and hit the corner of the coffee table hard. It's not always about a guy, Kaine."

"Maybe you shouldn't tease her about losing her job?"

"Agatha loses one a week. Usually, she doesn't care, but it must have bothered her on Friday," she paused. "She's gained a little weight recently, and it's made her more agile. Odd."

"Was the black eye worth it?" He took her chin in his hand again.

"Oh, yeah. Agatha is the instigator, usually."

"Do you always fight with your sisters?"

"Yes. It keeps them in line. I rule with teasing and small skirmishes. What did you do this weekend?" she asked as if she hadn't just called her siblings her underlings.

"I went to my sister's house."

"Did you see her son? How old is he?"

"He's three, and his name is Eddie." He kissed her neck; he'd missed her smell.

Pushing him away, she said, "I have to make supper. I'm late. I had planned to be here an hour ago, but Mom had to yell at us for borrowing her clothes." She rolled her eyes.

"The dress?" he questioned as she pulled out ingredients.

"Agatha squealed. She always does since she's Mom's favorite." She pulled the plastic containers from the fridge.

He grinned at her expression. "Good thing she gave you a black eye."

"I broke her arm last year, so I'm still ahead."

"How did you break it?"

"She wouldn't say 'uncle,' but I didn't think it would break. I think she was too skinny then. There was just nothing to her for a long time, but now she's putting on weight, and we're not saying a thing about it."

"What does she do?" He watched her mindlessly mix ingredients into the bowl.

"Artist, but she's a bartender for money," she said as if that paid bills, especially if she got fired a lot.

Harper looked over her shoulder at him. "What's your sister's name?" She tossed raw chicken into a bowl that had a lot of different spices in it.

"Arabella. She's younger than me by a number of years." He liked that her butt swayed as she washed her hands.

"Are you the oldest, then?" She turned back to him and opened another container that held vegetables already cut up.

"Yes, I have two younger sisters. But I don't speak with one of them, just Arabella," Kaine said. It had been years since he had seen his sister, who was actually his twin, but he was still the oldest. More years than he'd liked to admit had gone by since he'd spoken to his twin, but it was her choice, not his.

"I can't imagine not talking to my sisters all the time. Let's see." She stopped working and looked up at the ceiling. "I talked to them all today, or at least saw them all. Agatha was still moody."

"Your family might be unusually close since you all live together," he pointed out as she pulled out another big bowl and put in herbs and spices.

"Now we are, but once people start moving out, it won't be as easy to be close." She shrugged.

"I know what you mean. Once Arabella stopped working at the office, we floundered a little. But we just have to make a point of going to see each other. You won't have an issue, but maybe fewer black eyes," he teased.

She stopped mixing and looked at him. "I don't even notice it."

"I do," he admitted. His eyes went right to it every time. Also, he wanted to know if she had any more bruises or if the bruises from falling down the stairs had healed. It had been twenty-four hours since he had seen her and touched her.

"Then I won't show you my arm. *That* I notice." She chuckled and looked at her left arm that was fisting vegetables into the big bowl.

Getting up, he walked around the counter, pulled her arm away from the food, and looked at it closely. There was a three-inch welt on the underside, red and angry. He gently slid a thumb over it, but she flinched and pulled her arm away. "Don't touch it."

"What happened there? Another sister?" He looked at her other arm, top to bottom, but found no wounds.

"I burned it Friday afternoon on the oven." She watched at him looking at her arm.

Carefully, he lifted her shirt and pulled it from her body, letting it fall to the ground between them. He immediately began looking her over for more bruises or wounds.

"I have to cook," she said, but her voice was not overly demanding that he stop.

"I have to see how much damage the sisters have done and kiss all your new wounds." He kissed her eye and cheek that had a faint bruise on it. Then her shoulder, where he found another.

"I'm working," she reminded him as his hand unclasped her bra.

"Then take a break." His lips took her pebbled nipple into his mouth.

He knew she had stopped protesting when she moaned and grabbed his hair, even if her hands were damp from her work in the kitchen. Supper wasn't eaten for a long time, but neither said anything about it. What she made was amazing, but he couldn't decide if it was because everything she did was amazing or because she was a great cook.

CHAPTER FOURTEEN

Tuesday turned out to be long for Harper. Lucy showed up at Kaine's house at 9:30 a.m. to prep for the dinner party they were catering that night—well, Lucy was. Harper was taking off Wednesday because they had a corporate lunch, and they had a harder time getting waiters for lunch. Buzz and Maby were always busy for lunch.

Harper got up almost as soon as Kaine left because she had to clean the house before Lucy got there. Last week she had fired both the maids Kaine hired to clean his house. They didn't clean well, and there wasn't enough work for either of them. She would find a replacement by the end of the month, but until then, she would just clean before she left for the day. It was easy work, but she had less time this morning.

Last week Philip had quit, which had not been her fault at all. She had only slightly complained about his bad cooking and said he should want to work until Kaine came home from work every night, explaining that dedication to his food was what made a mediocre chef great. He had stomped around, complaining in French for hours, then he had thrown out her cookies—the ones she had made in her own kitchen on her own time. Sadly, she had let him have it—in French. It was a language he wasn't aware she spoke. After their argument, he had walked out of the house, and she had yet to see him again.

That left her little choice but to add making Kaine's supper to her day. It had been easy, and he didn't seem to notice. Nor did he notice that she was using his kitchen as her catering kitchen this week and the next one. The house kitchen was torn up completely, so Lucy came over to Kaine's house to make everything. It was easier than finding and renting a place for two weeks.

"I love it here," Lucy said, looking around. It wasn't the first time she had been there, but she always said it.

"I want to be home and cook in my own kitchen," Harper replied. She hated using Kaine's without asking, but she wasn't going to ask. He didn't know she had another job; that probably fell into the same category as having another man in her life. He wouldn't like it.

"Just another week." Lucy tossed all the ingredients she carried in on the island. "How are the maids this week?"

Lucy teased her about her almost lack of jobs, but she didn't mention anything about sex. She hinted and smirked about it but never said it.

"Fired them both. I need to hire someone next week. They were barely cleaning the extra bedrooms. They knew Kaine wasn't going in them."

"So, you're not going to stay and work for him? You seem to like it. And I'm killing it as a boss," Lucy said.

"Yes, you are. That just means we can start taking on two events next month." Harper walked behind her as she grabbed another load of stuff from the van.

"What? And give up all this to work?" Lucy handed her a container of raw pork chops.

"This was only a way to pay for the kitchen. You know that."

"But now you really like him, and he's hot and rich." She winked.

"He is hot, but rich doesn't matter. He works all the time, sometimes sixteen hours a day," Harper reminded her sister … and herself.

"So do you when you need to. He just has to find a reason not to do that. Could you be that reason, Harper?" Lucy pushed.

"No way. I'm just here when he gets home." Even if he started to be home around the time she was supposed to be back, she wasn't looking at that as a sign that he thought of her as anything but sex.

"Okay, Harper. Keep thinking that." Lucy tossed her a pair of plastic gloves.

It had been three years of working with Lucy. At first, she was just her assistant and flunky, but now they were equal in the business. Both could cook and keep things on task. Lucy just lacked the confidence to be the boss, but it was coming.

"I can bring everything back home when you go to the event. I have to bring Violet to Sera and Harrison anyway. Ag has a job interview, and Emma has a school thing, so I'll drop her off before coming back here to make something French for Kaine." Harper opened the pork packages.

"Okay, then I don't have to worry about all the extras in the van all night." Lucy started to peel potatoes.

By 2 p.m., Lucy was on her way uptown to the event, and Harper was heading across town to wait for her baby sister to get out of school. It was always odd that her baby sister was in the second grade, and she had been mistaken more than once as her mom.

At the house she had been raised in, she leaned against a pillar on the front step after changing clothes. She'd also grabbed two extra sets for Kaine's house. So far, her plan had worked great to come home almost every day, but with the kitchen a mess, her return visits to the house were becoming harder. Since Lucy was coming to the house every day, she sometimes brought clothes for her, but Harper was determined not to feel like she lived there. She didn't want to be comfortable in a world she didn't belong in. It was halfway over now, and she knew she was going to miss it when she was gone. She would miss him.

Spying the happy, black-haired little girl coming down the street, Harper went to greet her. She was the combination of her mom's bubbly personality and her dad's looks. The kid was adorable.

"Hi, Violet! Are you ready to go see your mom and dad at work?" she asked.

"Yep. Ag is busy today." Agatha was who usually took care of her after school and had since the kid was practically born.

"I know. Shall we toss your bag in the house and head out?" Harper tapped on the bag on Violet's back.

"No, I have homework I have to do. I'll do it in mom's office."

"Okay, then we can go." Harper loved that Violet loved school. It was something she didn't share with all of her siblings. Most were happy they no longer had to go.

After a quick drive downtown, Harper looked at the building she used to work at and didn't miss it at all. Okay, maybe she missed seeing Kaine during the day, but most days, she was busy anyway.

Parking two blocks from Sera's office, Harper helped Violet out of the car and took her little hand for the walk.

"Do you know which office is theirs?" Harper asked the little girl. She had been to the place a few times over the last few months.

"The one with the brown door," Violet said.

"Correct. Do you know which floor?" Harper asked. She wasn't exactly sure.

"Yes. What's your favorite color, Harper?" Violet asked, jumping off-topic.

"Yellow. Bright yellow like the sun. What's your favorite color?" Harper asked as they continued down the street.

"Today I like ice-blue. I really want to paint my room in our new house ice-blue. Have you ever seen ice-blue?"

"Yep. It's very light, right?" Harper smiled at the little artist. She knew she was artsy because she spent so much time with Agatha.

"Yes, I want it in my new room. At the new house, now that Mom has finally found one she likes," Violet said with a sigh. Sera had been against any house that wasn't the Lovely house until she'd found one two blocks away. It seemed two blocks was close enough for her to actually move out.

"Nelle?" The name made her turn around. She had gotten used to it over the last few weeks.

"Yes?" she asked and saw Kaine standing behind her.

She had watched him dress in the black suit this morning and had suggested the green tie, but after seeing it in the sunshine, she didn't know if she liked it anymore. Nor did she like the anger in his eyes. Anger focused on her.

"Who is this? You said you didn't have kids," he hissed at her.

"I don't have to explain what I do during my off hours to you." She didn't like what he was insinuating.

Violet grabbed her leg, and she knew she had to get the kid away from angry Kaine. Violet had maybe seen all her sisters fight each other, but she also saw that they loved each other. A strange man, not so much.

"It's okay, Violet." She patted her sister's head, then turned to Kaine and stated, "I will see you at seven, not before. That is the agreement."

"Why is he so mad?" Violet asked as Harper picked her up into her arms.

"I have no idea." Harper rubbed her back, trying to ignore Kaine staring at her as she walked away.

"You said you didn't have children, Nelle." He grabbed her arm, stopping her.

"*I don't*. She's my sister," she snapped at him, just as pissed as he was.

"You think I'll believe you have a sister who is, what, five?" He looked Violet over.

"I'm eight!" Violet yelled. She hadn't been raised with six loud sisters for nothing. "Harper's my sister."

"You tell him, Violet." Harper grinned at her. Nobody was ever going to push the little girl around. "I am your sister."

Violet wiggled free of her arms, yelling, "Daddy! This man is yelling at Harper. Make him stop."

Looking at where Violet was heading, she saw Harrison, who was glaring at them both as he picked up his daughter. "Harper has to yell at him herself, baby. He is her problem. The more I know, the more I'll have to tell your mom." Harrison turned and walked away from her.

"Damn you, Harrison!" She called after him, but he probably didn't hear.

"You lied about knowing Harrison?"

She shrugged. "We happen to have a mutual friend. He's only been dating my stepmom for a few months." She wasn't explaining her mom's baby daddy to him.

"The one he's engaged to and getting married to in a few months? But you barely know each other?"

"He doesn't spend a lot of time at the house. I didn't think he would remember me."

"But he did, didn't he? And you didn't say anything about it at the time."

"What of it?" She crossed her arms. "It hasn't affected what I'm contracted to do, has it? You don't need to know anyone in my family, do you? This isn't a relationship!"

"You're right. It's just fucking!" he hissed as she pushed past him back to her car. He had humiliated her in the middle of the street. Not since the beginning of the relationship had she felt dirty, but now she did. He had made it dirty.

CHAPTER FIFTEEN

BY THE END of the day, Kaine's nerves were on edge. Would it even matter if Nelle had a kid? It wasn't like she was going to be with him forever or that her having a kid had affected them being together since this all began. But for some reason, seeing her with a kid reminded him he knew very little about her, and since he couldn't ask, it was up to her to share. So far, she hadn't done a lot of that.

But now she was gone. No way was she completing the contract now, and he had no way of enforcing it.

As he pulled into the driveway, he saw there were lights on. She must have forgotten to shut them off when she'd left. He briefly wondered if she had taken her bedspread. He wouldn't be surprised if she had stopped by to grab it. Or maybe she would just leave it to remind him of what he had lost. It was the only thing she ever left here; not even her clothes were there during the day.

Opening the door from the garage, he saw her right away. She was leaning against the door jam, her expression blank as she looked him up and down. Her voice was flat as she stated, "Supper is ready when you are, Mr. Hawthorn."

"Nelle, you're here?" His happiness was instantly replaced with apprehension at her tone. What was she doing if she didn't want to be there?

Without answering, she turned and went to the kitchen, leaving him alone in the entry. After taking off his jacket and hanging it up, he followed her.

In the kitchen, she was taking a pan from the stove and dishing up a plate of something. Nothing Philip had ever left had been in a pan before. The house had an amazing smell of chicken and dill when he had walked in, but it looked like beef on the plate that she slid towards the stool he usually sat in.

"Can we talk?" He slid off his suit jacket as he sat on the stool.

"Your time is your money, Mr. Hawthorn." She grabbed a fork and knife for him. It seemed she wasn't eating tonight.

"I'm sorry. I jumped to conclusions about the kid. I was in the wrong there. Your personal life is your personal life. You were off, and I interfered in that." He looked at her folded arms and angry eyes.

"I have a life outside of this house. I didn't start living when I started this job. I have friends and family and a past that might intersect with the present. Every time I leave this house, you get angry and think I've done something. Not once have you just asked me about it. Scaring an eight-year-old going to visit her parents is not acceptable behavior," she said calmly, though her back was rigid as she stood by the stove.

"I wasn't trying to scare a little kid." Picking up the fork he realized he wasn't very hungry after all.

"Well, you did. Then I had to spend an hour trying to tell my mother why my boss was yelling at me in the middle of downtown in front of her child. How I could let it happen, and why I don't just quit. Because nobody needs that."

"Why didn't you quit?" he wondered, not for the first time since he'd walked into the house. There was no reason for her to remain working for him unless she wanted to.

"I signed a contract. I've already spent the money, and I have no way of repaying that amount back." Her eyes looked away from him. She didn't want to be there.

"I don't want you to be here if you don't want to be. But, despite everything, I would like you to stay, but only if you want to. Not because you think you have to."

"I can't stay if every time I leave this house, you lose your mind about something. You don't seem to trust me. I need trust, Kaine."

"When we signed the contract, you gave no indication you knew Harrison. I should have asked about your little chat before you signed the papers. What did you talk about?" He now realized his mistake about that. At the time, he had just thought that Harrison was talking to her to make sure she wasn't going to just sue him over any of it.

"I told you we have a mutual friend, and she happens to be my stepmom, whom he is marrying. I had to tell him not to tell my stepmom because she wouldn't understand why I would change jobs. So, I told her I got a bonus for working as your at-home personal assistant, but it included nights, weekends, and hours I wouldn't normally be working. I told everyone that." She shrugged.

"That's what you are; it's not a lie. How do you barely know the guy your stepmom is marrying and has a kid with?"

"Harrison doesn't spend a lot of time at the house. He thinks we're a bit wild. We don't see him much. The kids haven't even moved in with him yet, or Mom, really. They're looking for a house but haven't found anything they both like. Besides that, they've only been dating for two months, maybe less."

"And he's marrying her?" The man Kaine knew didn't seem like the "hurry up and get married" type. He had assumed they had been dating a long time and that Kaine hadn't known about it, which based on his workload, was entirely possible.

"You haven't met my mom." She shrugged as if that answered everything.

He slowly pushed the plate of cold, uneaten food away from him. "Are you leaving?"

"I'll think about it," she replied and pushed away from the counter.

Watching her walk out of the kitchen, he wondered what she was thinking. He had been an ass, both with the little girl and the redhead.

He was beginning to realize that he had to just assume everyone she spoke with was her sister; most of them were.

After cleaning the dishes and putting them in the dishwasher, he was happy with how Philip was keeping the kitchen cleaner than he usually did and that the dishes he usually made were now interspersed with new, better ones. The man hadn't contacted him in weeks about the menus, but Kaine was happy with them.

Shutting off the lights, he went into his office to get some work done, the work he hadn't been able to concentrate on earlier in the day. His mind had been on Nelle and the kid. Her having a stepmom explained how her sister could be so young and how someone so close in age to Kaine would be the father.

Kaine hoped that giving her time to think would be enough to get her to stay. He kept his ears peeled for sounds of her leaving, but they never came. The house was silent as he read a report Bex had emailed to him just as he was leaving work.

His executive assistant had found a way to work only eight hours at the office, and if she needed to work more, she did it from home. And that was limited. Maybe it was time to talk to her about exactly how she did it, because he knew his sister was the reason why she did it. Bex had found a way to put her family in front of her job, something that Kaine hadn't been able to figure out.

But now, suddenly, he wanted to spend more and more time at home with the woman who might be walking away from him that night. And if she did, he knew he wouldn't change anything. Her being in his house had made it a home, and he was starting to like his home.

CHAPTER SIXTEEN

HARPER HAD no idea what to do. Her logical side said to walk away —no, run away, but there was a whole other side that wanted him, even after everything he said. It was that side that was winning the battle tonight, not the logical, pissed-off side.

At this point, there was slightly over a week and a half left on her contract—not very much time at all. And then she wouldn't see him again. So why walk away early?

Even now, she couldn't just walk away from him and never see him again. She already missed him, already wanted to come back to him. She was already half in love with him, and that was *not* in the contract.

Next week her dream kitchen would be completed, and the entire operation would move back to the house, back where she wanted it. This morning she had looked over Kaine's kitchen and pointed out the five things she would change if it were her own. None of it would ever happen; it would never be her kitchen.

Kaine didn't want the distraction of emotions in his life, but her emotions were getting all tangled up in him. So far, she hadn't been able to reign them in, and she didn't know if she would be able to in the next week and a half either.

But she had to, and from there on out, she was a professional who didn't get emotionally invested in the guy she was sleeping with. She flinched, realizing that she hadn't been able to keep her emotions out of this business transaction. She had let Kaine's words hurt her because she cared what he thought of her. Before she could analyze it any further, she dialed her sister.

"Bea Bradford," Buzz said calmly into the phone. So professional, so grown up for her little sister.

"Can you talk?" Harper climbed into bed, pulling the yellow comforter around her.

"Of course, we can talk about that important bit of information. Excuse me, everyone, someone wants to talk to me," she said louder than necessary.

"Are you at work?" Harper didn't even know why she asked. Of course, she was at work, based on her tone and the way she was talking.

"I have to take this outside," she said in the same loud voice.

"Just talk to me when you can." Harper slipped from the covers and pulled off her jeans. She tossed them on the floor, deciding she would pick them up later … or not.

"What's happening? Aren't you and Luce at some fancy dinner tonight?" Buzz said. She must have gotten rid of her coworkers. Her usual half-annoyed, half-bored tone was back.

"Just Lucy. I took off tomorrow for the corporate lunch. Not as many helpers during the day. Why aren't you helping her?" Harper asked because Buzz was wasting her time as a reporter; she wasn't very good at it.

"Because I got stuck on gossip. Not even good gossip, but I had to work late. Agatha's working for me," Buzz answered.

"Thanks for getting your shift covered. I need to be there for every event," Harper said, looking at the ceiling.

"Hey, control freak, Lucy's doing great. This job of yours is exactly what Lucy needed. She had to force herself to just be the boss, no net. I think she's really blossoming."

"Blossoming? You've been a reporter for too long. I was just telling her today we could start doing two jobs at a time if we need to next month." Harper smiled. Their business was going to explode, which had always been her dream.

"Who will be your waiters, Harp? Your family is about done. Maby's dating a billionaire, and Mom is marrying a lawyer and will stop helping you at any moment. Agatha and I can't do it all. How about keeping your job with the ass and keeping the few-days-a-week schedule? Win-win," Buzz said, as if cutting back was even an option. They were about to take off. Not to mention her job with Kaine was about over.

"How is that win-win? Lose-lose is more like it, and my job isn't very secure here anyway. I should have quit today. We got into a little fight, and things were said." Harper held her breath.

"He's an ass. You just have to remember that. He's the same guy you were a personal assistant for at the worst hours ever, the same guy who's constantly working and being rude to you," Buzz reminded her.

Was he even that guy anymore? She couldn't think of him as that guy anymore, the one who never seemed to even see her when she was in his office.

"He's not that bad. When you get to know him, he's funny and easy to talk to. The night he yelled at you, he bought me pizza as a peace offering." Harper snuggled back under the covers and tried not to remember how gently he had made love to her that night, as if he were trying to make up for everything he did with tender touches and kisses.

"Well then, you must love him … and pizza." Buzz wasn't a fan of the food like Harper was. None of her sisters were except Lucy, and even she wasn't as into it as Harper. It had always confused her.

"No, not love," Harper said, but even she didn't believe it anymore. She had caught feelings for this guy somehow.

"You are so fucking in love with this guy!" Buzz yelled into the phone.

"I am not!" Harper yelled back on the defensive.

"Harper and Asshole sitting in a tree, f-u-c-k-i-n-g," Buzz sang as she giggled.

"Shut up, Buzz. I'll come over there and take you out," Harper threatened.

"You will not. You've been up since five or six. You're in bed, ready to crash," Buzz stated the obvious.

Her sister didn't even know about the emotional afternoon and was right. As usual, the day had caught up with Harper early.

"You're right. Bye, Buzzy."

"He has to be less of an ass if you think I'll approve of your love affair, Harps," Buzz said seriously, not something that Buzz usually was.

"It's not a love affair; he's my boss." She replied but was talking to air because Buzz had already hung up on her.

Shifting away from her love affair thoughts, she called Lucy to see how the event had gone. Usually, Lucy called at least once during an event, sometimes twice, but not today. Today she had been silent about it, which meant it was going great or so badly that Lucy was scared to call. Either could be the case, but somehow, she knew it was because her sister was finally comfortable enough to not need her, which Harper loved and hated at the same time. Letting go of control was hard.

Control was what she and Kaine had in common, and it was that control that was going to stand between them. Neither could let go enough for the other, which meant that this affair would end, and it would end quickly.

Pushing those thoughts from her mind, she dialed Lucy's number and listened to the ringing a few times before her sister picked up.

"How's it going?" Harper asked, no introductions or greetings.

"Great. One little flub with the hors d'oeuvres, but nothing to worry about," Lucy said. She sounded busy.

"Good. Tomorrow we start at six, right?" Harper didn't want to ask about the flub. Lucy could handle it and apparently had. No need to hash over it now.

"I will be there. I may be tired, but I'll be there. I was thinking about bringing Agatha with me if I can drag her out of bed. We could use the hands, and she needs the money. She didn't get the job she was interviewing for today," Lucy informed her, reminding Harper why she had been downtown with Violet today.

"Was her interview that bad? It was just today. Rejection usually takes a few days." She wondered if she should call her sister, except Agatha would hate to talk about it.

"I don't know, she just said it didn't go how she expected it to, so I left it alone. I didn't want to push and have her walk out on me. I needed her." That was how they had been treating her for months now: don't poke her, or she'll go into her room and never leave. It seemed to be getting worse and worse, but Harper hadn't figured out how to help her sister or what was even causing her to be so moody lately.

"Bring her if you can, and then you can sleep if we get a little downtime," Harper said, making a mental note to let her sleep no matter what.

"I am not sleeping in the bed you pleasure your boss in." Lucy chuckled into the phone at her joke.

"There are other bedrooms, Lucy," Harper replied a little too late. She had just admitted she was sleeping with her boss.

"Okay, 6 a.m.," Lucy said, not mentioning the slip-up, but Harper had just said it, and now it was public.

"Bye." Harper hung up quickly, as if that would make the conversation disappear.

Harper tossed her phone on the bed and groaned out loud. Lucy was now planning an entire day of teasing Harper for sleeping with her boss, just like they all said she was.

Staring at the ceiling, she knew that the bedroom was the one place they truly got along since day one. It seemed the further they got from this room, the less they got along. In the real world, trust was completely gone.

At this point, she wasn't willing to give up what went on in this room. It would be over soon enough, and then she would go back to her life and her new kitchen. Until then, she wanted to enjoy Kaine as much as she could.

CHAPTER SEVENTEEN

It was close to midnight when Kaine let himself stop working and see if Harper was still there. This afternoon, her sister and Harrison had called her Harper like it was her name. Her employee file said her name was Nelle Harper Lee Lovely, but she had never corrected him. In fact, she hadn't corrected him on the pronunciation until after the contract was signed.

But now, he couldn't think of her as anything but Harper. It suited her better and matched the Harp on her neck. Why she hadn't said why she had a harp on her neck, he didn't know, but he knew he should have pushed her about it.

He shut off the lights as he walked through the house, trying not to be happy that her shoes were still by the door, which meant she was either still there or had left her shoes. Either was possible.

As far as he could tell, the entire house was the same; nothing moved or was missing from anywhere. Not that she had anything but a small backpack of stuff in the house. He had been skeptical that she would live on only what could fit in there, but every day, she proved him wrong.

The bedroom was dark when he went in, hoping it wasn't as empty as the rest of the house. He saw her and could finally breathe again; he hadn't wanted her to leave. She had become a big part of his life over the last few weeks.

Since day one, he had started looking forward to coming home to her, seeing her, and talking to her. Even though she rarely ate, he loved sharing a relaxing meal with her and learning what little she would share with him.

After shedding his clothes, he slid into bed with her. This was another aspect of their relationship that had worked out better than he had ever expected. He had yet to see the docile, timid woman he'd thought she was. She was as active as he was in the bedroom, maybe more. She knew what she wanted and wasn't afraid to ask for it. Demand it.

That attitude of hers stretched into the other parts of the house. She was in control. There had been little things she had done that he barely noticed. One day, she had moved the living room furniture around. One day, she had changed around his closet, and another day, she had moved almost everything in the kitchen. Everything she moved seemed to make it function better.

He held his breath, hoping that he wouldn't wake her and have to fight with her again as he pulled her into his arms. In sleep, she moved easily and snuggled into his body, sighing as she did it. He lightly ran a hand over her body and knew this was the moment he would miss the most if she left ... when she left: her body tight against his as she slept.

It was after five when Kaine woke up the next morning. Rolling over, he realized Harper wasn't in his bed anymore. Her side of the bed was cold. With a curse, he quickly got out of bed to look for her, but if she was gone, she was gone. And he had slept through her leaving.

The sound of the shower got his heart rate down, and he realized she was already awake. Walking into the bathroom, he saw she was still in the shower, her naked body completely visible through the glass shower enclosure.

"I was going to wake you if you were still sleeping when I was done. You don't usually sleep this late," she said from the shower, her eyes on him through the glass.

"I don't, usually. Must have been tired." He leaned against the vanity, watching her.

"Today's my day off, so I won't be here when you get home. Did you need me to do anything before I leave?" She was washing her hair.

Without thinking about the day before and all that had happened, he pushed his boxers off and joined her in the shower. As he did, she said nothing but went willingly into his arms in the hot stream of water.

Hours later at the office, he could still feel her wet body against his. Tossing his pen on his desk, he looked out the window in his office and wondered what she was doing right then. Was she at least thinking of him?

He had to wait until after work tomorrow to see her again, which felt like a lifetime. His house would be empty when he got home. Tonight would be a reminder of what his life would be like when she was gone. How lonely it was going to be again.

Not for the first time, he wondered if she would make their arrangement permanent. The arrangement in itself seemed to be working out great, if he could keep the controlling aspect of his personality in check. She brought out a jealousy in him he didn't even know he possessed.

"Hey, boss. How's the weather?" Bex asked as she breezed into his office. Her eyes were on her phone, but it seemed she had noticed what he was doing anyway.

"Looks fine. Why?" He turned to her and noticed her black hair was shorter today. Not that he usually noticed, but it was way shorter than it had been yesterday.

"Because I didn't know you even knew there was a window there." Bex sat down, still looking at her phone.

"I look out it all the time." Kaine knew it was a lie, and Bex's raised eyebrow said it was also.

"Bella demands to see you and your woman tonight. She will not take no for an answer. It's getting hard to live with her when she needs to know everything about your life, and there are just parts of your life I don't need to know about or even think about. Could you just become a monk, so I don't have to talk to my wife about you and sex anymore?" Bex tossed her phone on his desk with a sigh.

"She's off today." Kaine couldn't not smile wondering how often Arabella asked Bex about his sex life. He was sure it was never.

"Tomorrow then. She'll just show up one day if you don't bring the woman to her. You don't want her showing up unannounced at your little sex house. Need I remind you that she has a key." Bex grinned.

"I'll have to ask her." He had no idea what she would say. Yes, he had met three of her sisters, sort of, but it hadn't been on purpose. Family introductions screamed "relationship" to him.

"Just tell her it's an event, and she can't say no. Not that I need to see her again. I've had a nice few weeks not seeing her. She's cute but very annoying. I can't see you two together; you're both so type A."

"She was always so meek and mild at work." Kaine looked at his assistant. They had such a different take on the same woman.

"In front of you, but shit, she was bossy. Her only reference was an HR director down the street. Seraphina Lovely is the nicest person you will ever meet. I thought with that reference, she must be great. *Wrong.*" Bex rolled her eyes.

"Her stepmom, then." Kaine realized how she got the job. "Harper, she goes by Harper. No, she doesn't seem to want to be a people person, but she doesn't have to be." Kaine folded his arms.

"What? Wait? Another name change? How many is that? I literally go by one name, and she gets three?"

"You go by Bex and Rebecca, except Arabella for some reason calls you Becca," He pointed out. He had never gotten the full story on the nickname thing. To everyone, they were Bex and Arabella, but to each other, they were Becca and Bella.

"That is different," Bex argued, but she couldn't hide her grin.

"She used Nelle at work, but her family and friends have always called her Harper." He liked to say her name. Harper.

"I'll continue to call her Nelle" Bex said, "And I'll tell your sister you will be there tomorrow evening."

"I should talk to Harper first," Kaine argued, not wanting to make plans. He already had plans for the first time he saw her the next day, and it involved staying at home and being naked.

"How about you call your sister then and tell her you don't want her to meet this woman? I'm tired of you 'hiding' her from Bella. She argued this morning that she's pregnant and should be getting her way on everything. Since she's carrying my baby, I let her," Bex said on her way out of the office.

As the door closed, he wondered what Harper would say about his tiny family. She had nothing but family everywhere. He had the three, and they had never given each other black eyes.

It was odd that her mom's name was Seraphina. Kaine hadn't heard that name too many times over the years and had never met another. It was the name of his twin sister, who had been gone for years now. She was married with kids somewhere out there, not needing Kaine or Arabella in her life.

It seemed Harper's mom was a better person than his sister ever was.

CHAPTER EIGHTEEN

THERE WAS no end to the dust in the house; it was everywhere. Gritty, grainy dust. The kitchen remodel was almost completely done. All that was left was putting in the additional stove since the new commercial fridge was already in the basement. It was up to Harper to clean the dust—well, Harper and Lucy, but Lucy wasn't exactly that much help with cleaning.

Harper dumped another pail of gray water down the sink and looked at her watch. It was only 4 p.m. She filled the pail again to keep working for another hour. She loved cooking and even cleaning after cooking, but not just cleaning.

Yesterday's dinner party had gone off without a hitch; they had even been able to clean up in the house instead of at Kaine's, though she had run over there at a little past five to make him supper. Then she had come home and had a night with her sisters, watching movies and eating Chinese take-out. It was fun to be with them all for a night, but when the TV was shut off and she crawled into her bed, she missed Kaine.

She shook her head to clear her thoughts, then took a pail of clean soapy water back into the living room. She removed all the stuff from the TV stand and washed away the grime that had collected over the years. Both Agatha and Lucy were home, but Lucy was sleeping, and Agatha was up in her third-floor layer, drawing. The house was eerily quiet. No one was yelling or arguing. She wasn't sure she liked the house like that.

Sera and Harrison were redoubling their effort to find a place of their own. Once one was found, the three would move out, and soon, so would Maby officially. Her engagement and pending nuptials hadn't made her admit she was moving out, and though she still maintained that she lived here and spent two nights a week in her bed, Harper knew she would soon move out as well. Then it would be four; half the population would be gone.

Then they would have to start making an effort to see each other and spend time together. No longer was everyone going to be around, even when you didn't want them to be. It would be more like they were never around, even when you needed them.

Like when it came to cleaning!

After setting all the knickknacks back on the stand, she started on the stairway railing. *Had anyone ever washed this?* she thought to herself. The rag came out black. The entire house was a disgusting bunch.

"Harps!" Lucy came running down the stairs in just an oversized orange T-shirt that said "srkd." Harper had no idea what it could have possibly meant, and she had never seen it before. "I just got a call from The J! Von Shild was canned! Day drinking! We're in on Wednesday!"

"The J! Wednesday?!" Harper's mind was racing, mentally changing her schedule for the next week.

"They're faxing the menu over. Do we even have a fucking fax machine? Because I think we need a fax machine!" Lucy squealed and danced on the landing.

"No need; it goes to my phone. How are we going to pull this off?" Harper stopped dancing suddenly as doubt started creeping in.

"With fucking pizzazz, Harp! We are that fucking awesome!" Lucy shouted at the ceiling and grabbed the rag from Harper and tossed it into the living room. It landed on the floor with a splat.

"I don't know if I can change my day to Wednesday. I already have

Monday and Friday off and am already leaving you short on Saturday."
Harper sat on the bottom step and sighed. Her job was getting in the
way of her career.

Lucy sat down next to her and threw an arm around her. "I can do
it; you know that. You'll have to help with the prep, and we can get
everyone else to help too. We can do it. Or you can just ask your boss
for another night off."

"We haven't been getting along very well lately. I don't know if
he'll let me," she admitted, though she knew she should just tell him
what was happening. He was a businessman, after all; he should
understand the pickle she was in with this new job. All she had to do
was tell him about it.

"Just try. We can do it. Everyone will chip in. We all know that you
need to work this month. If we're good, we'll be in at The J. This is
what we've been waiting for, working for. I knew that wedding last
month was going to be our in at that place." Lucy squeezed her hand.

"The J, Lucy!" Harper pushed all her thoughts of Kaine away and
focused on what was really important: Lovely Catering.

"You send me a list of what I need to add to the shopping list for
this, and I will contact everyone." Lucy pulled out her phone.

Harper checked her phone as well and saw it was after five. She
needed to get back to Kaine's and start supper. "I have to get home,
Luce. Let me know what you find out about everyone."

Lucy grabbed her arm as she got up from the step. "Home, Harp?"

"Slip of the tongue," she corrected, but it felt like home more than
this place had today. Even if that house had even fewer people than
this one, it had the one she wanted to see.

"I hope he's not the ass Buzz says he is. I don't want you in love
with an ass." Lucy let her arm go and went upstairs as Harper emptied
her pail in the kitchen again—the kitchen they would cook in for The J
in a matter of days.

After a quick change into clean blue jeans and a blue T-shirt with
"MY Ciyt" in gray on it, she headed across town to fix something
stupidly French for her lover. So far, he hadn't commented on the
improved menu or mentioned he knew she had fired Philip. Both left

her questioning his love of French food and how much the house staff had been getting away with and for how long.

Rushing in the door, she tossed her bag on the floor by the steps. She would deal with that later. She immediately headed into the kitchen, pulling out a saucepan before taking stuff from the fridge. The bonus of catering from Kaine's house was that she had ingredients here without bringing them from across town.

"You don't have to make anything tonight, Harper," Kaine's voice came from behind her, making her jump.

Bumping her head on the fridge shelf, she swore and shut the door, tossing a plastic container on the counter. "You're not hungry?"

"We've been invited to my sister's house for supper. I called Philip to say he wouldn't have to make anything tonight. He told me to talk to you about it."

"He quit. Not my fault," she defended herself, wondering what the chef had told him.

"I'm quite certain that it was mostly your fault. How long ago?" He folded his arms.

"The second week. He was such an ass. If you ever came home during the day, you would have known he needed to be gone." She opened the container of potatoes.

"And you've been cooking ever since? Even on your days off?" he questioned, watching her work.

She shrugged. "Yes, you like to eat. It was easy."

"You still barely ate. Most of the time, you don't." He was actually grinning at her.

"I'm a grazer. I eat all day." Harper finally relaxed a little. She had been worried about his reaction to what she had done. He had said she was in charge of the house, but she had been worried about how much control he would actually give her.

"Why didn't you tell me?" He walked closer to her and pinned her between his arms and the counter.

"Because it was only week two. Well, it was Monday, so still technically week one. He wasn't willing to change his hours to be here when you got done with work. At the time, I didn't think you would be impressed with me firing anyone." She gripped the counter, hoping to stop herself from touching him.

"Is that all?" He raised an eyebrow and didn't move an inch closer to her.

"He threw away my cookies and said I couldn't keep them in the kitchen. I have my limits, Kaine. *Limits!*" she would like to say it was his cooking that caused her to fire him, but it was more the cookies than anything.

He leaned down, and his lips brushed her forehead as he whispered, "You are so fucking cute. You fired my chef and then made meals for me for two weeks. What were you going to do when you were done?"

"I was going to hire someone. I'm working on it, but I haven't found anyone yet." She was relieved to see he wasn't mad about it.

"That's why you are in charge of my house. Because you're good at it." He kissed her neck as his hand wrapped around her waist, pulling her to him.

"Not mad?"

Instead of answering, he pulled her even closer and kissed her lips. She loved it when he just held her and kissed her. She let him lead and was surprised when he pulled away.

"We have to go to my sister's for supper, but I'll continue this later." He let her go and started to put the containers back in the fridge for her.

"Sister's? Yours? I didn't bring anything to wear." She loved her shirt, but not for meeting people in.

"It's fine; I'll change. They don't dress up for meals." He took her hand and pulled her from the kitchen, from her safe place.

"You could call and say I'll make something. That would be way easier for them," she argued as they went up to the bedroom.

"Nope. Eddie is better at their place." He let go of her hand to start taking off his suit.

Sitting on the bed, she was nervous. What did this really mean? She hadn't invited him to meet her sisters or mom—hadn't even thought about it.

"Are you sure your sister wants to meet me?" She watched him strip out of the suit and wished they weren't leaving the house. It had been an entire day since she had last touched him.

"Yes, since day one. I've been putting her off, but she's persistent. You'll like her; everyone does." Kaine was pulling on jeans. She had rarely seen him in casual clothes, but she was getting used to it. Very used to it.

"And her husband? Just as sappy?" she said, biting her lip, "Fuck, I said sappy. Mom's sappy."

"Her wife is not sappy. She'll take some winning over." Kaine pulled on a plain gray T-shirt, but his eyes were on her.

"Are you sure I can't cook? People like me better when I cook for them." She flopped down on the bed. This took more than a few hours to prep for. She had no time.

"They'll like you. Just be yourself." He took her hands and pulled her back up.

"Nope, I'm going to channel Sera." She smiled and nodded her head. "I can do that."

"No, channel Harper. It's Harper they want to meet. Not your mom."

"Can I invite Mom? She will talk and talk, and they won't even notice I'm there."

"Nope. Arabella will do enough talking." He pulled her to her feet and kissed her.

She grinned. "Can we just stay here and have sex?" She knew he'd like that idea.

"Nope, let's go so we can come home and have sex." He pulled her to the door.

A mile drive wasn't long enough to calm Harper's nerves. Maybe cleaning the house all day wasn't the best use of her time today. She should have been prepping for this.

Arabella's house wasn't as large as Kaine's, but not by much. Both siblings seemed to have done well for themselves. The house was cute and cozy despite the size. Walking up to the front door as Kaine held her hand, she marveled at all the flowers surrounding the house.

She was sure if he let go, she would bolt. He must have thought so, too.

Kaine knocked on the door, and Harper looked at him. *Who knocks?* Even when she didn't live in the house, she never had to knock. Maybe because it wasn't the house they had been raised in. But over the last week or so, Lucy had been working at Kaine's with her, and she hadn't knocked once.

When the door finally swung open, Harper could tell the woman was Kaine's sister, not the wife. This was a younger female version of Kaine: blonde hair and blue eyes. She was tall like Kaine, but not as tall as he was. She was wearing a flowing skirt that went to her bare feet, and her blue blouse made her eyes stand out.

"Kaine, you brought her!" the sister said with an excitement Harper did not feel. "I'm Arabella, and you must be Harper. I love that name—it's better than Nelle. I just love it."

Harper couldn't speak; Arabella had said it all. When she'd gotten herself together, she said, "Thank you. I'm lucky to have a nice middle name."

"Very. Mine is April." She shrugged and hugged her brother, then hugged her. "Becca left work a few minutes ago, so she's on her way. It seems her boss snuck out early."

Harper caught the not-so-subtle hint that Kaine was the boss in question. Now she wished she had paid more attention to who worked at the office because she couldn't remember any Beccas at all.

"I had to have a meeting with my house assistant," Kaine said, resting his hand on her back.

"And what was the meeting about?" Arabella's eyes twinkled with just-contained laughter. Harper wondered how much his sister knew about them.

Kaine didn't take the bait. "The chef."

"Can you believe he wastes his money on that? He could just have a restaurant deliver, or there are catering services for that."

"Some will even cook in your kitchen." Harper looked around the house. She could tell there was a kid somewhere; toys were everywhere.

"I hadn't heard that." Arabella looked at her with Kaine's eyes.

"Yup, you just have to look around. Some don't have the kitchen to make a meal to bring it, but they can do it in yours." She shrugged, not thinking about what she was saying as she looked around the house. Well-lived-in and nothing on display, just comfort. So unlike her brother's house.

"They don't have a kitchen?" Kaine asked.

"Not a commercial one. You need commercial to cater," she said as Bex Carter walked in from the back of the house. Becca was Bex, and Kaine hadn't told her. Maybe he actually was mad about the chef thing because he really should have told her.

"Becca, Kaine finally brought over his Harper. Her name is Harper now." Arabella turned to her wife.

"I see that. Hello again, Nelle," she pronounced the "E". They were not going to be friends.

At that moment, Bex was distracted by her wife wrapping her arms around her. The most annoying woman Harper had ever met melted before her eyes at the action. She smiled and returned the kiss Arabella gave her.

"Hello, Bex, or is it Becca?" she asked. If the woman was going to play this way, Harper had six sisters who had taught her how to do battles with just words.

"It's Bex to you. How has Kaine been treating you?" Yup, she knew about the entire thing.

"He's been treating me very well. It took some time to learn what his likes and dislikes were, the ebb and flow of the house, and its staff. But once I figured it all out, I was able to anticipate his wants and needs. The house has been running like clockwork, and the sex is *amazing*." She said a silent thank-you to the sisters and mom who made talking about sex easy.

Kaine laughed beside her. "Well, that's out."

"I have a feeling it was never hidden," Harper said to him.

"Since we know Kaine's great in bed, let's get some drinks and loosen up." Arabella shook her head at them as she let go of her wife and went further into the living room.

"What does the shirt mean?" Bex pointed to her.

Looking down because she couldn't remember which one she had on, Kaine guessed, "NY City?"

"Yes, NY City. My sister has dyslexia, but before she was diagnosed, she had a T-shirt business. We kept the mistakes. I think everyone just wears them when we aren't dressed up."

"Kaine said your mom was Sera Lovely? Isn't she a little young to be your mom?" Bex stared at her as if she were lying to Kaine about her mom.

"I really never think about it. She's been Mom for so long." She chuckled.

"You two are not very similar."

"Nope, I like to be similar to nobody. It makes me special," Harper stated.

"You're special, alright," Bex said, and Arabella shot her a look that made her lean back in her chair and shut her mouth.

"Sera's her stepmom," Kaine told the room. "She's engaged to Harrison Dean, my lawyer."

"I hadn't heard that. Is it recent?" Bex asked.

"Yes, and the wedding is the Saturday after Halloween, but not Halloween-themed. Mom actually hates Halloween, so one of us older girls has always taken the littles around the neighborhood," Harper explained.

"Who are the littles?" Arabella asked, leaning forward.

"Emma and Violet. Emma is fifteen, and Violet is eight. They're Mom's love babies." Harper took a drink of her wine and wondered how this unconventional family thought of a family of women barely related all living together.

"Love babies. I like love babies." Arabella giggled at the term. Sera had first had the one love baby. When Emma was three, she had even answered to "love baby."

"If you love that, you're going to love that the little one's referred to as the couch baby when she's not around. She was conceived on a couch at a Christmas party." Harper loved her mom, who kept almost nothing to herself.

"My babies are clinic babies. I like love babies." She tapped her stomach. "I'm just going to call them that."

"Twins?" Harper sat up.

"This time, yes. Boy and girl. They run in our family. Kaine's a twin." Arabella pointed at her brother.

"What? You never said anything. I have sisters who are twins." She looked over at the man she had lived with for weeks. He told her nothing.

"You two would definitely have twins," Bex said sarcastically.

"Probably not," Harper glared at her. "I don't think the twins and I share a father. The gene's probably not in me."

"Interesting," Arabella said. "Why not?"

"Just a feeling. I don't think any of us are actually my father's child. I think he knew, and that's why he didn't care to stick around. Not that he wasn't wetting his wick elsewhere." Harper drained her glass. Why was she even talking about this? She never talked or thought about her birth parents, ever.

"Dads are shit," Arabella said in agreement.

"That they are," Kaine agreed. "So, what's for supper?"

Harper was glad the depressing topic was changed to discuss the lasagna Arabella had spent the day making. She and Eddie had done it.

He put his arm around her. "Italian. Harper loves Italian."

"I like variety, not just French." She pushed him.

"Harper's a food snob," Kaine told them.

"A *foodie*. I like good food," she explained. Kaine made her sound bad, and all she wanted was to make a good impression on his sister.

"She lived in France for four years," he said, sounding oddly proud she had traveled.

"What did you go there for?" Bex asked.

She grinned her fake grin at her old boss. "To become a French chef."

"What happened?" Bex pushed.

Her smile quickly turned into a glare. "I became a French chef." She knew Bex didn't think she was ambitious, and the truth was that she hadn't been in the office. Her focus hadn't been being a good assistant.

Before Bex could answer, Harper's phone rang. Looking at the screen, she saw it was Lucy. She excused herself and went to answer it in what turned out to be the kitchen.

"Luce? What's happening?"

"Mom's out. She and Harrison are going to the event we're catering."

"So, she'll be there if there's an emergency," Harper stated, counting her as an option if things went to shit.

"Ag and Buzz are in, but Maby said Cliff is probably taking her also. My Cliff is taking her to a fancy dinner," Lucy said, and Harper could tell she was grinning.

"We have to hire some people. Maybe four." Harper started planning. She looked around the kitchen. It was white, and she could smell the lasagna in the oven.

"I've got two in mind already. I worked with them at the bar. We'll have to pay well, but they won't need to be trained. I'll ask around and see what I can get."

"You're kidding? Already? You are the best, Lucy. Maybe you don't need me at all." Harper grinned, loving that Lucy was taking charge.

"Nope, you're the boss." Lucy laughed.

"Then stop acting like a boss. I sent you the list for food. When are you getting it?"

"Monday afternoon unless I can con a sister into it on Saturday, maybe Mom," Lucy rambled as she thought.

"Take Ag. She needs to get out of the house. Has she said anything about the job hunt?" Harper asked as Arabella came into the room and caught her looking in the fridge. Innocently, she shut it and pretended she wasn't snooping.

"I don't think she'll go. Something's up with her," Lucy said, echoing Harpers thoughts.

"I know. I have to go, though. See you tomorrow."

"Yeah, love you."

"Love you back." She hung up and looked at her phone. She should call Agatha.

Out of the corner of her eye, she caught Arabella watching her. With a smile and a shrug, she said, "Family drama."

"At least Kaine and I don't have that."

"I don't know what life would be like if someone wasn't in crises at all times." Harper sat down on the stool near her. "When are you due?"

Arabella grinned and said, "Next month. Well, in two months, but they will come early."

"Have you come up with names yet? That's the fun part," Harper replied.

"You mean the hard part. We barely agreed on Eddie. We talked about it for months, and she had no opinion. Then when he was born, she suddenly knew exactly what she wanted to call him. She had wanted that name from the beginning and wouldn't tell me. Right now, we're thinking Ridge and Molly," Arabella said, not sounding convinced.

"They don't go with Eddie," Harper pointed out, not what the woman wanted to hear, she was sure.

Arabelle sighed. "I know."

"Are they Carters or Hawthorns?"

"Carters."

"If I have kids, I think I'll go with two first names. Gives them options in the future."

"Like using one for a while then changing?" Arabella looked at her pointedly.

"I have almost always been Harper. When I started working for Kaine, I just gave up correcting people. It didn't matter anyway since I wasn't staying forever."

"And after you changed jobs?" she asked politely.

"It went from professional to personal quickly, and it was odd to ask Kaine to call me something else." She shrugged, not wanting to explain her reasons for keeping her life separate.

"I told you they were hiding from us," Kaine announced, coming in from the living room.

"We should have worked harder on our hiding spot," Harper said to Arabella.

"Next time, we'll try harder." Arabella looked into the oven.

Kaine sat down next to her and grabbed her hands in his. Looking down at his hands holding hers on the counter, she wondered again why he had brought her to meet his sister. Since Bex was there and hated her, Arabella would never like her. Couples were that way.

By the end of the meal, she was no closer to figuring out why she was there. Over the past hour, nothing had changed, except Eddie thought she was fun. Of course, he had no control over his parents' opinion of her. As they said their goodbyes, she hoped this was their last visit with the couple. Arabella was great and easy to get along with, but Bex? Not so much.

But in the end, it didn't matter. Her time with Kaine was limited. Once the month was up, he would be done with her and would probably find someone else to fill her shoes. Thinking about him with another woman was painful, physically painful.

CHAPTER NINETEEN

Saturday found Kaine waiting again for Harper to come home from her day off, but this time, she was late. It was almost 7:30 p.m., and he had requested that she be home early. They had another event that night. This one was closer to home, but the meal had already been served, so there was no need to go anymore.

It wasn't that the event was even important. It was just that he had asked her to come home early, and she hadn't. She hadn't known it was important to him.

It was just after five that he realized he didn't know her cell phone number. He'd never needed to contact her. Until today, she had been on time or early every day.

Pacing the living room, he checked out the window to see if her Jeep was there yet. As he looked out, a red Jeep drove into the driveway, and Harper got out of the passenger seat. She waved at the driver, and the Jeep backed out again, leaving her to walk into the house alone. Today she was carrying a bag that he assumed held a dress and her backpack.

Her blonde hair was once again upswept from her face and was held in place by a clip, but some tendrils had escaped and were floating down her back and side. Her usual smile was missing, and she was biting her lip as she closed the door behind her.

Meeting her at the door, he saw she had black streaks all over her clothes and face. Her fingers were delicately holding the top of a metal hanger. Whatever was in it was hidden behind her back.

"Where were you?" he demanded as she hung the hanger on a doorknob, leaving most of the bag in a heap on the floor.

"I-94, trying to fix the Jeep. Mom thinks the alternator went out. I need to wash my hands." She held them up, and they were greasy black, as was her once light blue "HOsh" shirt and jeans.

"You could have called." He folded his arms over the tux shirt he still wore.

"I would have if I had your number, and your receptionist doesn't give that out. I got Agatha to pick me up and bring me here. What time do we have to be there?"

"Six." He wasn't taking her excuse as real.

"Sorry. I left there at four and then spent over an hour trying to fix the car. I usually can. Then I had to walk to get a signal for a ride. Agatha and Violet brought me here. Everyone was scattered this evening. Date night." She shrugged.

"Three hours along the side of the road, and nobody picked you up?"

"I do not get into cars with strangers, Kaine. Really, you would rather me be dead than late?"

"No, I would rather you drive a reliable vehicle that doesn't break down." He knew it was unfair of him to argue about her choice of vehicle, but their Jeeps must break down all the time.

"Are you paying for it? Because I have no money. I like not having a car loan to worry about every month.

"I just gave you a large amount of money, Harper."

"*Gave* me? How kind of you to give it to me. And I am generously donating my time to you and your house. For the last two weeks, I have cooked your every meal, cleaned this house from top to bottom with no help, attended functions with you, and fucked you whenever you wanted it. I earned every fucking cent of that money, and you got by cheap."

"Aren't you so overworked?" he stated sarcastically. Almost everything she did, she didn't have to. It, had after, all been her who had fired all of his staff and had yet to hire anyone.

"Fuck you, Kaine! I work just as many hours as you do. Hell, I work more. I haven't had a fucking day off since I started this job." She pushed past him.

"And what have you been working so hard on?" He followed her as she went up to their bedroom.

Before he could get there, she slammed the door behind her, not answering his question. Finding the door locked, he considered leaving her alone since she was in his house, and she apparently wasn't leaving. She wasn't going anywhere, but their argument wasn't over either. Anger won out, and before he could stop himself, he kicked in the door and marched into the room they had shared for almost three weeks.

The bedroom was empty, and he found her in the bathroom calmly washing her hands. The noise from the door didn't seem to affect her as she didn't turn away from the sink. Stopping in the doorway, her calm demeanor stifled whatever he was going to say. Instead, he instantly tempered his anger. "I was worried, okay? I had no way of contacting you. I don't have your number. I didn't know if you were hurt, and I was scared you were hurt."

"You didn't act worried, Kaine. You acted like I did it on purpose. I don't know why you can't accept that there are things I cannot control. I was out on that highway for hours! I didn't want to be there. I was so fucking lucky Agatha picked me up; everyone else is out. I came as fast as I could. Lucy even did my hair." She didn't turn from the sink, but he saw a tear roll down her cheek in the mirror.

Walking up behind her, he shut off the water and wrapped his arms around her, pulling her back into his body. "I'm sorry I acted like an ass. I'm glad you're safe. I never want you to be alone on the road again."

"You are an ass." She didn't pull away, but neither did she lean into him. She just stood still.

"Thank Agatha for me when you see her, for bringing you to me safely." He kissed her exposed neck as the smell of gas and oil assaulted his senses, but not enough to overshadow the smell he would forever associate with her: lemon and vanilla.

"She said you would probably be an ass." Her eyes were watching him in the mirror.

"She's right. She gets that from her big sister, who's always right." He kissed her neck again. Her body was finally relaxing into his.

"Don't treat me like a child, Kaine. I know you think I'm immature, and in some ways, I am. But you didn't grow up in my house. Judith walked out when I was eight, and she wasn't around much before she left. I was babysitting the younger ones alone by the time I was seven. The day Dad walked out on us, I was fifteen. He was gone for over a month before any of us got worried—that's how used to being alone we were. Sera lets us be kids again, and maybe we still are in some ways. But we're all still responsible women and take our careers seriously, even when others don't."

"Harper, I don't treat you like a child." He knew he did.

"We don't all live at home because we are lazy. I know you think that. We live at home because it's never lonely, and you know you belong there. On Saturday and Sunday mornings, we all gather in the kitchen and have breakfast together. We catch up on everyone's week, and nobody judges." She chuckled and leaned her head back on his shoulder. "Actually, everyone judges."

"You've missed that when you're here?" He pulled her tight to him.

"I haven't missed many. If everyone comes on Saturday, we don't get together so much on Sunday. And they know I'm working." Her body finally melted into his.

"You can spend any time you want with your family, Harper. I don't want to get in the way of that." His eyes met hers in the mirror.

"Thank you, Kaine. I sometimes miss being at the house. There's so much I do miss." Her wet hands covered his as she said it.

"I don't want you to miss a thing with them, but I also want you here with me." His lips went to her neck, staking his claim on her.

"Then don't think I'm not trying to get back here to you. Things just happen. Things I can't control," she whispered as she watched him kiss her.

"I'll try. Let me make it up to you tomorrow. I'll take you anywhere you want to go." They both watched his hands slip down over her breasts.

Her eyes caught his in the mirror again. "Anywhere?"

"Wherever you want to go to eat, but you have to eat." His fingers slipped down to the hem of her shirt and pulled it over her head, revealing the fact that she wasn't wearing a bra tonight.

"I will," she whispered as his hands smoothly encased her naked breasts.

At this point, she still had grease smeared across her face, and her hair was still falling from the hairdo her sister had done for her, but she was gorgeous. He couldn't take his eyes off her. Though he didn't know what dress she had brought, he knew it had nothing on her topless in his arms right now.

There was no way he was moving from this spot with her. Their eyes met in the mirror as his hand slipped lower and unsnapped her jeans. He was waiting for her to stop him, but instead, she subtly rubbed her ass into his erection. At that moment, there was no stopping until he had her bent over the sink begging for more. And watching the entire time.

CHAPTER TWENTY

Her demand had been that it be fancy enough to wear the dress from the night before and not French. To her delight, he'd brought them to The Detail. It was new, and it was packed. How he had gotten reservations, Harper didn't know. Bex had most likely been involved, and she wasn't letting thoughts of her in tonight.

For weeks, she had been reading about this place in Buzz's paper. Nothing had been written by Buzz about it yet, but soon. It was the in place to be in town, even if you weren't really anyone.

A fancy meal didn't make up for the hours lost on the highway only to be yelled at by him once she finally made it to his place, but it was a start. With luck, they wouldn't have a fight by the end of the meal. Her hope was to save that for when they got home. Because fighting during sex was a turn-on.

This time she had asked Sera for a dress, and she had been given the blue one. It wasn't her favorite, but it would work. It wasn't as tight as the red one had been, but it wasn't exactly loose either. She was hoping tonight he would peel it off her and not just end the night in a fight.

Slipping into the matching shoes, she was lucky she and her mom were basically the same size. The twins were also about the same size, so sharing clothes had been a constant for many years now. Why buy a little black dress when Lucy already had one, or a new jacket if Maby wasn't using her old one anymore? Though with both Sera and Maby moving out soon, most of their clothes would be moving with them.

"Are you about ready?" Kaine was leaning against the door frame, looking her over. She had requested that he wear his navy-blue suit, and he looked as gorgeous in it as always.

"I think so. Do I look okay?" She tried to clasp the necklace she had brought to wear with it.

He grinned as he watched her struggle. "You look gorgeous, and you know it."

"Please, I hope to just be presentable." She missed as she tried to get the tiny pieces to fit together.

Walked to her, he took the necklace and clasped it with ease. "I should have made you put this one on last night; then I would have already peeled you out of it."

His lips were on her neck as she replied, "If you're quick, we won't be late."

Pulling her back into him, he said, "It will not be quick when I take this dress off of you. I'll need to kiss every inch that is exposed, then touch it. Slow enough to make you beg me to take you."

"Oh." She leaned back into him, wanting to begin the exploration.

"We have to go." He backed away from her, and she instantly missed his touch, even if he took her hand.

Not giving her a chance to talk him out of leaving again, he helped her into the Porsche. The short drive was quick, and she looked out the window as they drove past the spot she was stuck at the day before. Her Jeep was gone; the garage she had called had taken it sometime yesterday. She hated letting someone else work on it, but Mom was a lawyer now, and Agatha wasn't coming out of her room much.

"I need Wednesday and Saturday off next week," she said as she looked at her phone and schedule. It would be better if she could take the entire week off. They were booked solid, and Lucy was going to be so busy.

"We have an event on Wednesday." He downshifted as they turned off the interstate.

"I can't. I'm so busy that night," she replied, tapping that day and looking at the menu that had come through, along with a few more odd requests that only The J could ask.

"Sorry, it isn't something I can get out of." He looked at her.

"Okay, I will need…" She looked at her calendar again. Nothing was as important as the night at The J. It was their chance to show them what they could do. "Tuesday night."

"Okay, that works."

This way, she wouldn't have to wait until 10 a.m. to start prepping. She could get up early and let Lucy sleep in or do something else.

"Are you okay with that?" he asked, touching her leg.

"Yeah, just planning things in my head. Don't mind me." She tapped more on the phone.

After pulling up to the restaurant, Kaine handed the keys to the valet as he led her into the busy restaurant. She had been planning her order since Kaine had told her they were going to the restaurant this morning. The chef was supposed to be amazing.

It took less than five minutes for them to be seated. It had been so long since she had been out in a fancy restaurant. In reality, she didn't like it. She'd always found the food lacking for the price you paid for it. It was the excitement of being there that she liked.

"Looks like you might like it, Harper." Kaine teased her from across the table.

"I will love it, I swear." Even she could hear the doubt in her voice as the waitress came to their table.

After placing their drink order, they were silent as they perused the menus. Harper closed hers and looked at him in the dim light. He was as good looking as he had been at the office with that suit on. Possibly better since he was going to go home with her today. And would for another week.

"Do you know what you want?" he asked over his menu.

"Yes, I knew this afternoon. I glanced at the menu then." She placed her chin in her hands, elbows resting on the table as she watched him look over the menu.

He closed his menu. "Did you want to pick something for me?"

She grinned. "Sure."

"You're not going to look at the menu?"

"No, I know what to get you already. I know what you like."

"And what is that?" He set the menu down on hers.

"To have stayed at home."

He laughed at her response and said, "You do know what I like: you."

Laughing at that, she took a long drink of water, stopping herself from telling how much she liked him. Somewhere along the way, she had fallen in love with the man, a man who felt nothing for her and never would. He didn't want to feel anything for her, which was why there was a contract. Once it was over, he would be gone from her life forever.

Picking up her water glass again, she drained it to take the edge off the sudden chill in her heart. When the waitress came, she asked a few questions about other menu items, then ordered what she knew they would enjoy.

After deciding that she was going to enjoy the last week with him instead of dwelling on the end of it, she asked, "Did you talk to Arabella this week?"

"Yes, she's holding her own with the babies. They're due in a month, and she's torn between excited and terrified."

"I can see that. The exit route is scary, but you get a baby in the end. Or two." It sometimes seemed odd that none of her sisters had ever had a baby, condoms or not. They had all been sexually active since high school, and not one slip-up.

"Do you want kids one day?" he asked, his blue eyes were on her.

"Yes, one day. I really have spent more time thinking about *not* having kids over the years than having them. But with Violet growing up, we don't have the baby in the house anymore. Now that Mom is getting married, maybe she'll have another. Or Mabel, now that she's actually marrying Cliff." She shrugged. Who knew where the next baby would come from?

"Not the reporter?"

"Buzz? No, well, probably not. I don't see Buzz bringing home a baby. Not yet, anyway."

He tilted his head slightly. "Buzz? I thought her name was Bea?"

"Buzz, like the sound a bee makes. She's always been pretty flighty." Harper watched the appetizers arrive, stopping their conversation.

As she sampled them, she analyzed how they were made. She looked up to see Kaine staring at her. Shrugging, she went back to her examination.

Kaine smirked. "You said you were going to like it."

"I like it, but I would like it better if there was more salt in it. Maybe we got a bad batch." She took another, but only opened up that one also.

"None of that, Miss Lovely. You are going to enjoy the food, not pick at it. No complaining," he reminded her.

"What if it's truly bad?" At this point, she didn't know if she could enjoy the food no matter what.

"All the reviews are good, Harper. If it's that bad, you can complain all the way home. But we're not stopping for pizza on the way." He took her hand in his.

"What if I say please?" She grinned at his cocky smile.

"Maybe then we can stop." He took another appetizer and put it on his plate.

With a swirl of green, the seat next to her was suddenly filled by a red-haired reporter. "Just pretend I belong here. And if the ass yells at me again, I will go ballistic on him. I don't care about making a scene."

Bea Lovely was glaring at Kaine, daring him to say anything. When he didn't, she turned back to Harper with a smile. "How's it going?"

"Good. Are you being chased out of a fancy restaurant?" Harper asked, handing her the small plate with the two disassembled appetizers on it.

"Not anymore. I'm with someone with a reservation." She started to eat the food. "Where were you last night? Thought you were going to The J again? I didn't see you there."

"The Jeep bit it on I-94, and I spent hours out there until Agatha picked me up." Harper watched a Maître D glare at her sister, but they didn't approach the table.

"How's she doing? Still in her room?" Buzz asked.

"Yes, as much as she can. I think she went to that new place by the Blaze yesterday. Not sure, though," Harper said. Her mom had told her the day before.

"I heard that place was going to be good. We should go when it opens, especially if Ag is working." Buzz took two more appetizers. "These are good. Can you make these?"

Harper folded her arms. "I can, but I won't."

"I would eat them." Buzz took another one. "I think Luce and I are doing karaoke tonight around midnight if you want to ditch the boss. We can have the band back together again."

"I bet Mabel isn't going out, so the band isn't back together," Harper pointed out. They all would sing with enthusiasm, but none of them could sing.

"Cliff is not going to miss a chance to sing to his lady love." Buzz took Harper's wine from her and drank it.

"Mabel isn't going out tonight. She has to work tomorrow, unlike all you fools. Besides, I'm working." Harper frowned at her sister and took her glass back.

"Oh, it looks like it, Harps." Buzz snorted a laugh then recovered, shooting a glance at Kaine.

"Looks a lot like you." Harper shot back, daring her sister to say anything else about it. The sisters had gotten bolder about what they would say to her about her job.

Buzz turned to Kaine. "Ass, can Harper have a few moments off to sing some eighties country songs with her sisters?"

"Beatrix, I'm sorry I was mean to you when we met. Harper forgot to inform me you were sisters," Kaine said.

"She shouldn't have to tell you. We look exactly alike," Buzz answered with a straight face, as they both did when people said they didn't look alike. Even Violet would tell people they look alike now.

"I know," Kaine agreed, "except the hair and the eyes and the height thing."

"She doesn't look so large until she's by me, but you get used to it." Buzz shrugged.

"If Harper wants to go out singing with you, she can." Kaine's eyes said he wanted her to himself, though.

She didn't get time to answer before their food came, distracting everyone. Then everyone's attention turned to what Harper had ordered for them. Even Buzz spent time commenting on the dishes and how good they looked.

They ate in silence as Buzz finished off the appetizer, and then Harper filled her small plate with some of her meal. Kaine did the same, making it hard for Harper to breathe. In that moment, the last part of her heart was gone. Kaine had gone from hating Buzz to feeding her.

"Are you coming out then?" Buzz asked when their plates were empty.

"No, I'm not in the mood." Harper couldn't think of a better response. *I want to have sex with my boss* just didn't sound right.

"Kaine, get her more wine, and she'll be in the mood. Better yet, pour some tequila in her; that really loosens her up." Buzz turned to the man, her words nearly making him laugh.

"She's working, so I don't want her drunk." He didn't look at the redhead as he said it.

"She's a fun drunk." Buzz grinned at him, then turned back to Harper. "Are you coming home tomorrow? We should take Agatha out for lunch."

"Lucy and I are going to the grocery store," she told her sister.

"You two can sure live it up. I have to go see if I can get anyone to talk to me." Buzz looked around the room and finished off Harper's water.

"Good luck, Miss Bradford," Kaine said to her as she got up.

"I don't need luck, Mr. Hawthorn. I need a fucking miracle right now." Then she was gone, weaving her way through the room to see who she could see.

"Sorry about Buzz." She pushed her plate away, ready to be yelled at. Buzz had stayed at the table longer than she had expected her to. It just showed how much she wasn't enjoying reporting.

"I liked seeing you talk to her. You're very concerned about your sisters." The waitress gave him the bill as he talked.

She shrugged. "I'm the oldest; it's my job."

"If you want to go to karaoke with them, you can. I don't want to stand in the way of your sister time."

"Nobody's showing up anyway. Buzz will be stuck here most of the night, Lucy has to get up early tomorrow, Maby works tomorrow, and Agatha is in her room right now." She held up a finger for everyone as she listed what everyone was doing.

"So why ask you then?" Kaine leaned back in his chair.

"If I had said yes, she would have rounded people up, I'm sure. But I don't want to go out tonight. I have other things to do."

"Should we get out of here and get to those other things?" Kaine stood up and took her hand.

"I don't see any reason to stick around here." She let him lead her from the restaurant and out into the chilly night.

On the car ride home, Harper let the warmth of the car encircle her as she tried not to look at him driving. She didn't want the end of their contract to get in the way of their last few days together. *Just enjoy this time*, she demanded herself. It would be over soon enough, and she could be depressed about it then.

CHAPTER TWENTY-ONE

LEAVING HARPER ALONE in his bed had been harder this morning than any other morning since they had started to sleep together. It was after 7 a.m. before he got to his desk, and he was glad his morning personal assistant was new, so she didn't know how late he was. But the extra hours with Harper Lovely had been worth it.

After seeing her with Beatrix on Sunday, he realized that the Harper who lived with him was the real one, not the one who had worked for him for a year. He had wondered often who she really was but now knew she was relaxed and outgoing and would speak her mind no matter what, just like her little sister.

Now that he knew the real her, he was finding it hard not to fall for her. From her devotion to her family to her picky eating habits, she was irresistible.

But today started week four of their contract. They needed to talk. He needed her to know that he wanted her in his life, not just in his house and bed.

"Pretty soon, you'll just be working eight to five like a normal sap, Kaine." Bex breezed into the room.

"Shut up, Bex," Kaine barked at her.

Bex sat down in her chair. "Did your girlfriend leave?"

"No, but I don't need to be criticized for coming in later than usual." Kaine tossed his pen on the desk.

"Not criticizing, just observing. Heck, I'm happy you've found something that takes you away from work. An interest that gets you away from this desk. You were working yourself to death."

"I was not. I don't get everything done that needs to get done as it is," Kaine pointed out.

"Hire people. Ever thought about that? Then you can spend time with your lady love." Bex smirked at him.

"I don't trust anyone," he reminded her and regretted his words when she flinched.

Bex sat up straight and tossed her phone on the desk between them. The woman had worked for him for years, even before she fell in love with his sister. He trusted her more than anyone else in the building.

"You had better learn, Kaine, that women don't like their men to work eighteen hours a day. They get tired of being alone," Bex stated, bringing up his ex-wife. "And though you don't like to admit you want a woman in your life, you do. You, in fact, want one woman in your life, and she is not going to put up with you going back to working constantly."

"I need to work. And Harper and I have worked so far."

"You mean the last three weeks? Because that is no time, in another three months, she'll be gone if you keep it up. Why do you think I only work eight to five? Arabella wants to see me. She knows that sometimes I have to work when I get home, but when I do, I usually wait until Eddie is sleeping or Arabella is busy. I choose my wife over my job. You need to think about that," Bex stated.

"Harper is not my wife."

"Wife, girlfriend, lover, it doesn't matter. You have to make time for them, or they'll think they don't mean anything to you. Claudia felt that way; that you didn't love her enough to make time for her," Bex replied bluntly.

"I loved Claudia," he hissed.

No longer did he think he was still in love with her, though. In fact, he hadn't even thought about her in the last month. Not that he was in love with Harper, but he was definitely enjoying his time with her and wanted more.

"Not enough to want to keep her. You've liked this one from the beginning and have only worked later when she was off. Since day one, she's been worth that hour of your time. What does that tell you about your feelings for her?" Bex smirked.

"I am not talking about my feelings with you."

"You don't have to. I know them already. I know a Hawthorn in love, and you are in love with this one." Bex leaned over the desk and glared at him.

"I'm not in love with her. What we have is a contract that we are both finding very satisfactory." Sure, he really liked Harper, but it wasn't love, not even close.

"That nonbonding piece of paper you call a contract has nothing to do with why she stays or why you want her to. I know what you're going through, Kaine. I fell for someone and didn't want to. I wanted to fall for someone, don't get me wrong, but not your sister."

"What's wrong with my sister?"

"Absolutely nothing. She is perfect in every way. But at the time, I let my image of her cloud everything I knew about her. I let her get away because I didn't think I could work with you and love her at the same time."

"What does this have to do with Harper and me?"

"I had all these ideas about who Bella was and who she wanted in a partner. Just like you do with Harper. Or actually, you and your lack of wanting someone."

"What changed your mind?"

She shrugged. "I talked to her. We decided what we had, the connection, was worth taking a chance on. It was worth getting to know each other for."

"You got married within weeks of starting to date her."

"What can I say? We're magic in bed, and I got her knocked up, which forced my hand, so I did the honorable thing and married her." Bex always said that, and though it sounded like a joke, it wasn't.

Arabella was pregnant when they got married, and Eddie looked more like Bex than a Hawthorn. Kaine chose not to ever question it.

"I still don't want to know how that happened." He put up his hands in hopes of stopping her from further explaining.

"No way am I letting you in on how to please a woman in bed, Kaine. There are lines we're not going to cross." Bex winked. "But it seems you do okay, according to your mistress."

"Can we just talk about something relating to actual work?"

"If you must," Bex said and picked up her phone. "On second thought, I'm going home."

"What?"

"My wife is asking me to come home." She didn't even look at the screen before pocketing it.

"Is it the babies?" He sat up, concerned.

"Not everything is about our children, Kaine. Sometimes it's about spending time with my wife. And it's just about nap time for Eddie." Bex winked at him again, and he tried to ignore her.

"Go then, but let's agree not to talk about it." He waved her off.

"Agreed." She grinned and walked out of the office.

Picking up his own phone, he checked for any messages from Harper. He could use an excuse to leave early, to spend time alone with her. Except it was her day off, and she deserved a day off. He just wished he knew what she was up to.

CHAPTER TWENTY-TWO

HARPER FELT like old times as she crawled out of her bed at three in the morning. Shuffling to the bathroom, she was happy nobody else was up, so she didn't have to wait. One advantage of living with Kaine was no lines to the bathroom. After a quick shower, she headed down to the kitchen to start prepping for tonight. She just wished she could be there for the actual event.

When Kaine said she was working on Wednesday, she had picked Tuesday to get an early start on the prepping and let Lucy sleep and relax more today. Tonight would be stressful enough for her since Harper couldn't be there.

Not that she had even bothered to ask where they were going, she just knew she had to be there on time this time. She couldn't even pretend there was something wrong and drop in on The J since her truck was still being fixed. No excuses at all.

Tonight's menu consisted of both beef and chicken. They already had the chicken marinating, but she had to get the beef out of the fridge to season before getting it in the oven by 5 p.m. Since the menu had already been set, the meal was different than their usual. They could not change anything, but they could make it all better than before.

By 10 a.m., every sister who could help was. Even Sera had taken the day off after feeling guilty that she wouldn't get to help tonight. With so many hands, they were getting everything done so quickly, she had even told Lucy not to help anymore. Lucy would have to take over for her at 4 p.m. with way less help.

"So, Lucy gets to sit, but I have to roll these little suckers?" Agatha asked from the table, where she was making an appetizer.

"Yes, she is working tonight," Harper said and showed her again how to make them correctly—which Agatha barely paid attention to.

"I'm working tonight," she protested and tried again.

"Not as much as Luce. She has to make sure you're not throwing these little suckers away after you spent so much time making them."

The kitchen was hot, but Agatha was wearing an oversized sweatshirt and sweatpants. Everyone else was in shorts or leggings and T-shirts, not that Harper was going to say anything about it. If Agatha went to change, she would never come back.

"Where are you going tonight?" Lucy asked from the table where she was reading a magazine—or trying to. Lucy couldn't read well due to her recently diagnosed dyslexia. Now at least she understood why she had difficulties and was working on learning what she had missed over the years.

Harper hugged her partner in crime on the way past her. Lucy knew all their recipes by heart, even when Harper had to look up some every once in a while. Lucy didn't have that option, so she'd memorized everything the first time. The articles Harper had read on her sister's diagnoses made perfect sense.

"I forgot to ask," Harper admitted. "I was so concentrated on everything happening at The J tonight that I couldn't think about what I was going to be doing, just on what I wanted to do."

"Don't you have a week left?" Sera asked, sitting down next to Agatha to help her roll.

"Five days," Harper said, wishing for more time, way more time.

"Harper is in love with him," Buzz said from the counter. Oddly, she was eating cake and not helping at all.

"I am not."

"Harper and Kaine, sitting in a tree," Buzz sang cheerfully as the others joined in on the "f-u-c-k-i-n-g."

"Thank you, everyone, but he's my boss," she reminded them.

"You are so cute, Harper. What does he look like?" Sera asked with interest.

Buzz jumped in with a description, one that wasn't very accurate in Harper's opinion. "Blond hair, blue eyes, tall. Not overly cute."

"His name is Kaine? Hawthorn?" Sera asked.

"Yes, and he's a workaholic and likes French food. But we've been working on that," Harper added.

"Do you have a picture?" Sera asked.

"No, I guess I've never taken one," Harper replied, knowing she needed to at least take his picture before she was done. To have a reminder of him for the future.

"His house is gorgeous. We should be doing this there." Lucy closed the magazine.

"We have a bigger oven now, Lucy, and more refrigerator space," Harper said.

"But he has more granite, way more."

"So, who needs a dress tonight? I'm starting to think we need to invest in a dress shop," Sera said as Maby, Lucy, and Harper's hands shot up.

"I think I have to just start buying dresses. Or make Cliff buy them," Maby suggested, because he was a billionaire, so he could afford it.

"I'm about done with events with dress requirements," Harper told the group since she had only five more days left that she would be working for Kaine and going places with him. After that, if she were going to a fancy event, it would be as a caterer. No dresses needed for that.

"I can get by with your extras, Sera. I can't buy myself any." Buzz sounded depressed. Her career was not taking off, and it was now getting her down.

"We should each get one when we go looking for bridesmaid

dresses. Then we'll have a good rotation," Mabel decided. Only Sera actually got excited about the idea.

By 4 p.m., Harper and Lucy had loaded up the van, and Buzz, Mabel, and Sera were getting ready. Harper still hadn't had a moment to get ready. Her day was packed until she was supposed to already be ready and waiting on Kaine.

Buzz brought Harper's dress down from her room as she headed out to Kaine's for her last event with him. She hoped she would be able to let go of control of the dinner elsewhere so that she could enjoy her time with Kaine tonight, but she was afraid thoughts of The J would consume her.

After rushing into the house, she noticed that he was already there. Glancing at the clock, she saw that it was almost 5 p.m.

"I'm almost ready!" she yelled as she ran up the stairs. Never was she so glad that Mabel had stopped her an hour before and pinned up her hair. The others gave the hairdo a six out of ten, but it would be good enough.

While pulling off her dirty clothes, she realized she forgot to grab an extra outfit before leaving home, which meant she would have to wear them home tomorrow. She hadn't planned to go there, but now she would have to. Pulling on the yellow dress, she knew her mom had her wear it because it was her favorite color. Her mom knew that the evening would be stressful for her, so she did everything she could to make it a little easier.

Harper rushed down the stairs without even putting her shoes on. He was already waiting at the bottom of the stairs. Waiting, but not angry like she had suspected he would be. Maybe he was learning to trust her.

CHAPTER TWENTY-THREE

The dress looked like it was made for her that night, all light and airy with a color to match her personality. She was a vision coming down the stairs, her bare toes peeking out on every step.

"Sorry, I'm late. I tried." She stopped and put her shoes on when she got to the bottom. Her hair was up again, but this time, her tattoo was visible. Tonight, she was all Harper.

"It's fine. We're not late yet. Did you purposefully dress like our bed?" Ever since the yellow bedspread had shown up, he really had thought of it as their bed.

"Nope, my mom dressed me. She's not aware what the bed looks like." Her eyes twinkled as she said it, knowing he was thinking about them in that bed. Which he was.

"She has amazing taste in clothing." He pulled her to him and kissed her. She smelled of pot roast and cinnamon, an odd combination, but he couldn't get enough of it.

"Harrison does. But once they're in her closet, they're hers. And today, she was happy to share." Pushing away, she turned in a circle for him to admire her.

"I will have to thank him the next time I see him." He took her hand to lead her to the car.

Across town, they pulled up to The J, and she gasped, "We are *here* tonight? Perfect!"

"I thought that you would want to come back here since you liked it the first time."

"I've been dreaming of being here tonight for a week. Thank you, Kaine." She kissed him and bolted out of the car.

Handing off his keys to the valet, he barely caught her as she walked into the party. Even though it was early in the evening, the room was almost full of people. Nobody was missing this event. Finally catching up to her, he gently grabbed her arm so that she didn't get away from him again. He would never find her in the crowd, even in the yellow dress.

"Everything looks good," she said, not really to him.

"It always does in here." He saw her red-haired sister rush their way. She did seem to be everywhere.

"Harps, you're here! I haven't seen Maby yet, but Mom is some-where." The redhead looked around her, but she was so short, she must have seen nothing.

"I'll find her eventually," Harper replied, not as concerned with everyone's whereabouts.

"Are you eating with us again, Beatrix?" he asked her as he roped an arm around Harper's waist.

"Nope, no eating for the press. But I'm stuffed anyway; I ate all day. Lucy made cinnamon rolls late this afternoon," she said and hurried away from them.

"Are you not hungry either?" he whispered in her ear.

She giggled. "I'm too nervous to eat."

"What are you nervous about?" he questioned.

"All this. I have to run to the restroom." Pulling away from him, she hurried away, stopping a waiter as she went. The black-haired woman took an appetizer and licked it, then handed it to her. He was sure she was going to reject the food that was offered. Instead, Harper took it with a laugh and popped it into her mouth, eating it without hesitation or even analyzing it. He wondered what was going on with her tonight.

Within minutes she was back and breathless from her rush, but her eyes were twinkling with excitement, more than the last time they had been there.

With her arm in his, they slowly moved around the room, chatting with friends of his he rarely saw anymore. Most he hadn't missed. After the first few, Harper had gotten into the conversations and would chat about just about anything, always making Kaine look good. She was amazing at small-talk, even if her eyes were constantly darting around the room.

"Kaine, is that you?" a sultry voice asked from behind him.

Turning, he looked into the dark eyes of his beautiful ex-wife. She was still as good looking as when he had met her on campus at the university. He had fallen hard for her then and hadn't stopped loving her since she'd left him.

"Claudia," he responded back to her, Harper's hand still held tightly by his.

"I can't believe you're at a society function. You hate these," she said. It was true—he did hate them, but he had to attend some sometimes.

"I'm trying to reform him, but he's a hard nut to crack," Harper interjected herself into the conversation. Over the last hour, he had learned there were very few conversations she had nothing to say about.

"Oh, I know." Claudia looked Harper up and down, more up since Harper was at least five inches taller than his ex was.

Kaine introduced them. "Harper, this is my ex-wife, Claudia Horn."

"Mrs. James Horn?" Harper asked as if she had heard of her. "Nice to meet you."

"Yes, I am. Nice to meet you also. Harper, is it?" Claudia loved that Harper seemed to know who she was.

"Yes, it is." Harper grinned. She ran out of things to say, so her eyes shot to the waiter with black hair and give her a pointed look.

"So, how have you been, Kaine? How long have you and Harper been an item?" Claudia wasn't very subtle.

"I'm fine, and Harper and I have been an item for a while."

"A while? He's so cute. Well, you don't think so anymore, but he is. We've been living together for months. I think this will stick." Harper laughed and held on to his arms. She was laying it on thick, and it seemed Claudia was buying every word.

"How are you finding time to date with all the work you put in? He's a workaholic," Claudia replied to Harper as if it were a little secret only she knew.

"Not so much anymore. He's really cutting back now that we're together. He finds it hard to get out of bed in the morning, and he has been known to even come home early a time or two." Fuck, she was good. It was all true.

Claudia's dark eyes narrowed at her. "Give it time."

"I think with time, he'll be home even more, especially when we start having children. He won't want to miss that." How had she even guessed that Claudia had left him because she wanted a husband to have kids with? Not that she and James have had any children yet, and they'd been married a few years now.

"Well, Kaine deserves happiness." Claudia didn't mean it. Kaine knew the woman enough to know that. "Is that Clifton Scott the fifth?"

Both he and Harper turned to where she was looking. Kaine had no idea who Clifton Scott was, but by Claudia's tone, he was rich, and she wanted to know him better.

"I think it is," Harper said from beside him.

"I've been trying to get an invitation to that wedding for weeks— social event of the year. But with the engagement so short, invitations are hard to come by," Claudia replied.

"We should talk to them then," Harper said and yelled out, "Cliff!"

Dozens around them stopped talking to look at her. For her part, she didn't notice, just waved the man over. To Kaine's surprise, he and his date changed directions and headed their way. He hated that Claudia was getting her meeting because of Harper. Claudia didn't deserve a meeting, and he hoped that she didn't get an invitation.

In a matter of minutes, he had started seeing his ex-wife in a whole new light, and it wasn't flattering. Sure, she was still beautiful, but the beauty was only skin-deep. Maybe even less than that.

"Kaine." Clifton dropped his date's hand and took his in a big shake and half-hug, as is they had met before and were already friends.

"Cliff." Kaine tried to sound as confident, using Harper's nickname for the man.

"It's been a while; we need to get together. Did you get the wedding invitation?" Cliff was grinning from ear to ear as he looked at Kaine, ignoring Claudia completely.

"I did. It's coming fast." Kaine had no idea, but if Claudia were scrambling for an invite, it was coming up.

"I know, but once you fall for a Lovely lady, you get her off the market as soon as possible." Cliff laughed as if it was a joke. For her part, his fiancé said nothing but rolled her eyes.

"Oh, Clifton. Mabel Lucie, this is Claudia." She stopped and looked at his ex. "I cannot remember your last name."

Claudia's jaw almost dropped. Harper had just been gushing over the woman and now claimed she didn't know who she was. He knew it was killing his ex inside.

"Horn," was all Claudia said.

"Nice to meet you," Cliff said quickly, then turned his back on the woman and looked Harper up and down. "Looking good tonight, Harper."

In a huff, his ex-wife grabbed her husband, who had said nothing the entire time, and dragged him away. No way was she putting up with being ignored, even if she wanted a wedding invitation.

"She's gone," Mabel Lucie said from beside Cliff. "Stop acting like an ass."

It was the first words she had said, letting her fiancé do all the talking before. The woman looked familiar, but Kaine couldn't place where he had seen her. Someplace recently that he knew.

"I was acting like you're supposed to act here," Cliff said, then turned to his fiancé with a grin. "Help Harper out, gorgeous, or the world will see those nipples. Not that she cares all that much."

All eyes went to Harper's dress, and the girlfriend rushed over and grabbed the dress by the top and pulled it up, shaking them a little. She then let it down and did it again, this time laughing. Then Harper grabbed hers and did the same thing.

"I can't get them to stay in," Mabel Lucie grumbled to Harper about her chest.

Cliff was beside him, not suppressing a chuckle as he had his phone out and pointing at them. "Keep going, ladies. Sister action is hot."

"God damn you, Clifton Scott!" His girlfriend dropped her sister's dress and turned on him, slapping him across the forearm that was holding the cell phone in a blue case.

Kaine looked from one sister to the other and saw the resemblance, realizing where he had seen her before. It was the sister who had given Harper the shoes from weeks before. These two sisters looked more alike than the redhead looked like either of them. They were both tall and had the same eyes, which were glaring at Cliff. He was happy he wasn't a part of the joke.

"I got a picture, Kaine. I can send it to you." Cliff's eyes didn't leave his fiancé's.

"That's my phone," Mabel Lucie said and grabbed it from his hand. Opening it, she cursed at him again. "You put my case on your phone. Why?"

"Because it would piss you off. It worked." Cliff took the phone back from her.

Harper punched Clifton Scott in the arm and said, "Cliff and Maby, this is Kaine Hawthorn."

"The ass?" Cliff asked.

"My boss," Harper stated, folding her arms.

"Maby? I thought your name was Lucy?" Kaine looked at her again. Maby was the one whose Jeep Harper had gotten a speeding ticket with. It had been a name all this time, not an adverb.

"Mabel and Lucy are identical twins. Different people altogether," Cliff informed him with a wink, and added, "You have a nice house. I was thinking Maby needed something like it."

"When were you at my house?" Kaine looked at him in shock, kind of wishing his ex was there to hear their conversation. She'd thought their house wasn't good enough for her anymore.

"I picked up Lucy a few weeks ago. Don't worry, I didn't take anything." Cliff slipped his arm around Mabel.

"Have you seen Mom yet?" Mabel turned to Harper, who was looking around the room again.

"Nope, probably ditching to make out with Harrison. Those two." Harper laughed, and both Cliff and Mabel joined in.

"I have to run to the ladies room again," Harper said and took off before anyone could say anything about it. Cliff was called away, and Mabel followed with a small wave. It seemed Harper's sisters were everywhere, and one was marrying very well.

"Kaine, you're here? I didn't think you were going to be here tonight. Harper must be crazy right now." Harrison Dean came up behind him as he waited for Harper to return.

"She's in the ladies room, again," Kaine said to his lawyer.

"Yeah, the ladies room. She isn't a control freak for nothing," Harrison mumbled, but Kaine heard him and wondered where else she would have gone. "Now I want to introduce you to my fiancé, Sera."

Kaine turned to her, smiling at the woman who had captivated Harrison Dean. She was in the red dress Harper had worn. It was a perfect fit for her mom. Unable to speak, he just looked her up and down. Her blonde hair was swept up into an elegant bun, and it looked the same as it had years before. In fact, she had barely changed in fifteen years. Still as blonde and bubbly-looking as she had when they were eighteen, the last time he had seen her.

At the time, he hadn't known it was the last time he would see her. She had been packing to go to university, just like him, but he was heading to Chicago, and she was going locally. He hadn't even bothered to hug her as he said bye and headed out the door. It had always bothered him, not hugging her. By Christmas, she'd been in Indiana and married to a man he had never met.

"Kaine," she smiled at him as if it had only been yesterday that he hadn't hugged her goodbye. "When Harper said your name today, I wondered if it was you."

"Where have you been?" he asked, still in shock. Anger was bubbling to the surface.

"You two know each other?" Harrison asked, pulling his fiancé closer to him, sensing a threat.

"Harrison, stop. Kaine is my brother." Sera sensed it too and explained.

At once, it hit him: she was Harper's mother. His sister was her mother. All the years she had been missing from his life, she had been raising Harper and her sisters. Here in the city, not in Indiana like his dad had told them when she'd left.

"*Brother?*" Harrison looked at him and then her. They didn't look a lot alike, but her and Arabella did, now that they were adults.

"Well, he was. I was disowned for marrying Bradford. I would have been disowned anyway for being pregnant, so I let it happen. I haven't seen Kaine since we went away to college in separate towns. I had always thought you would stay in Chicago." Sera turned to him as if they were just school friends catching up.

"I was for a while, but Arabella needed me, so I moved back," Kaine explained to his long-lost sister. *Nothing strange about that.*

"How is Arabella? She's the twins' age," Sera said, not really to anyone in particular.

"Good, married with a son and two on the way," Kaine informed her, not filling her in the particulars of their sister. It was up to Seraphina to want to know more.

"I have seven girls." She grinned at her accomplishment. "Only two are mine, but I get them all."

"That's what Harper says." He didn't want to remind her he was dating her daughter; hell, he wasn't really dating her. He was just living with her and having sex … with his stepniece.

Just as she'd said the words, a yellow dress appeared beside him. Her eyes went to Sera, and she said, "Mom, you're here! I can introduce you to Kaine."

"No need, Harps. I already know him," Sera replied to her.

"Harrison introduced you then. That's good," Harper said, assuming what had happened.

Sera smiled. "No, I knew him before that. He's my brother."

"I thought you didn't know anything about your siblings." Harper stared at her in shock, a shock he was feeling also.

"I didn't until right now."

"Well, this is awkward." Harper looked from one to the other. He wished he knew what she was thinking, but she was looking around the room again when she asked. "What is Cliff doing?"

Everyone started looking where she was looking, and Harrison said, "Being a waiter?"

Beside him, Harper pulled out her phone and put it to her ear. "What is Cliff doing?" He watched her listen and then hang up.

"What's going on?" he asked in confusion.

"Half the desserts were forgotten at home, and Agatha and Mabel are getting them. Cliff is filling in for Agatha. *Shit!*" she hissed.

"It's okay, Harps. Lucy has this. It'll all turn out." Sera reached out for her and patted her on the back.

"No, it's not. I have to go," she told Kaine and rushed off. Watching her practically run, he had no idea if she was upset about him being related to Sera or whatever her sisters were doing. It seemed the sisters were up to something.

"She tried, I guess." Harrison shrugged.

"I will go get her. Lucy really is doing okay. No need for two cooks in the kitchen tonight." Sera headed off in the same direction as Harper, but at a slower pace.

Watching them in confusion, he had no explanation for what was happening. Then saw the redhead moving through the crowd with purpose, also converging on the kitchen.

"So, are you in on the crazy Lovely train forever?" Harrison asked.

"I don't even know how crazy it is. I haven't met many of them," He admitted.

"Tonight will get hairy, and you're not man enough to keep Harper from that kitchen. She isn't called a control freak for nothing. But

Lucy can handle it; this month has been good for her." Harrison crossed his arms.

"What's Harper going to do in the kitchen?"

"Do you ever talk to her?" Harrison asked in shock.

"Yes, she likes food, but I don't think the caterer wants her in the kitchen."

Harrison laughed at him and slapped him on the back. "Lucy and Harper *are* the caterers. What did you think she did on her days off?"

"I don't know. I couldn't ask," he admitted, but Harrison already knew that. It was in the contract he wrote.

"Lucy has had to take over a lot of the work, but I know Harper did a lot of the cooking still. I couldn't believe she wasn't going to be here. Harper's dream has been The J for months now, according to Sera," Harrison said.

Suddenly, a lot of things came into focus: why she was never hungry, why she always went home, why her two days off were never the same days, and why she was exhausted when she finally got back. And why she always smelled of food, even when she had worked in his office.

And now he knew why she had wanted today off—because they were catering here. They must have worked all day to get ready for tonight, and for him, she was willing to not be here. Or was it for her job?

Leaving Harrison, he wandered to the kitchen and saw Mabel come out in a black dress that hugged her curves.

"Mabel?" he called after her.

"Do you see Cliff?" she acknowledged him and asked as she scanned the room.

"I haven't seen him in a while."

"If you see him, tell him I'm changing and will be right back." She then turned and went back into the kitchen, leaving Kaine looking for the man.

Scanning the room, he spotted Cliff across the room. He was happily handing out hors d'oeuvres with a woman with black hair. She was the one who'd licked the appetizer Harper had eaten. The man his ex thought was important enough to need an invite to his wedding was a waiter right now.

Kaine couldn't wrap his mind around this evening. All he wanted to do was take Harper home and peel that yellow dress off of her, and now she was his quasi-step-niece and a caterer. It was like his world had completely turned off-kilter. He had no idea who she was.

CHAPTER TWENTY-FOUR

HANDING Agatha another tray of desserts, Harper was glad the evening was just about done. Buzz and Lucy were already washing dishes, and Cliff and Maby were drying or arguing.

The meal had gone off without a hitch, except that Kaine was now fully aware that she had a second job. So far, she hadn't seen him, just heard about him. He had stayed for the meal, sitting with Harrison and Sera per Buzz, and he was now talking with some old dud, per Agatha.

At this point, she was a little disappointed in herself because she should have just left the event to Lucy. Her little sister had it covered when she had walked into the kitchen; even the desserts were on their way. But Harper had taken over, and Lucy had been pushed back to second in command, a role she seemed more comfortable in.

"Harper, Kaine asked if I could give you a lift to his place, or home, whichever you preferred." Sera breezed into the kitchen. She had successfully refrained from helping all evening, unlike Harper, who had tried, but only just barely.

Looking up from dishing double chocolate cake, she said, "I think I ruined your dress, Mom."

"Honey, you might have ruined more than a dress tonight. I think you should have told Kaine you were a caterer." Sera leaned against the counter.

"He doesn't like when his employees have a second job." She tried to play him off as her boss, not the man she had fallen for.

"But you always had it," Sera reminded her.

"It's fine, Mom. My contract runs out in three days anyway." Harper tossed down the fork she was lifting out cake with.

"That was your job, Harper. I don't think it's a job anymore." Sera managed to see through most of her kids' bullshit.

Instead of talking about herself, Harper leaned against the counter and turned it on her stepmom. "Sera, he's your brother. How did that happen? You got me the job."

"I didn't put two and two together. I never saw him and didn't know he owned the company. I had just heard about the job last year. HR talk. And I haven't seen him in fifteen years. When my parents disowned me, he and Arabella were included on their side, not mine."

Covering her face with her hands, she said, "I had sex with him. My uncle, I guess."

"Harper, yes, he is my brother, but you are my daughter first. And he makes you happy."

"Still your brother!" Harper said, looking at the floor, wishing she still didn't want to be with him.

"I'm going to tell you something that I haven't told any of your sisters, ever," Sera said.

"You are my favorite? You say it all the time to every one of us."

"You are all my favorites, but no. Kaine is lucky to have found any of my daughters because they're the best women on the planet." Sera laughed at her own words.

Harper groaned. "Cheesy."

"Go. Harrison will take you wherever you want. I'll help the girls clean up." Sera pushed her out of the kitchen, knowing Harrison was taking Harper home tonight.

"I'm going," Harper argued as she was pushed into the dimly lit room, one she hadn't been back to in over two hours.

Harrison was just outside the kitchen, waiting for her. She joined him, and he escorted her to his Volvo. So far, Sera hadn't made him buy a Jeep. It would happen soon.

For most of the drive, they were silent. Harrison didn't even ask where he was taking her, just drove towards Kaine's house. It seemed he knew her better than she had thought.

"Your month is about up. What then?" Harrison didn't look at her.

"I don't know. We haven't talked about it."

"I haven't been told to make up a new contract, and I won't if asked," Harrison stated as he exited the interstate.

"I won't sign another if that's what you're worried about," Harper replied, looking out the passenger window. She wondered if she really wouldn't sign again, this time more eagerly than the last. She wanted another month with Kaine no matter how she got it.

"The contract was never enforceable, Harper. We all knew that the day you signed it." Harrison pulled into Kaine's drive.

"I know," she said, but she was still willing to do it, maybe even for more than a kitchen.

"Then only you know why you signed it."

"I don't know if I did," she lied.

He eyed her for a moment and said, "Keep telling yourself that, Harper," as she slid out of the car.

Watching him back out of the drive, she wondered if this was a mistake. Kaine was pissed at her. She had ditched him for another job. But he ditched her all the time for his job, so why was hers any different?

No matter what, she needed her stuff from his place. She would just grab them and head home. Her Jeep was there anyway.

She was a little surprised the door was unlocked, even though she wanted it to be. Still in the yellow dress, she had no key and could have been stranded on his front step until morning. Inside the house, she kicked off her heels by the door and slowly climbed the stairs to their bedroom … his bedroom.

The door was open as she slipped inside. He was lying on his side, facing away from her, sleeping. His blond hair was messy as always, and his bare shoulders and chest were visible above the yellow bedspread.

Nothing indicated whether he wanted her there or not. Her clothes were now folded and put in a dresser drawer, which he always did when he found them on the floor. Her bag was on the chair she always tossed it on.

Undecided on her next move, she gasped when he sat up in bed. His eyes looked her head to toe in the moonlight. Slowly, he got out of bed and padded over to her with bare feet.

Stopping in front of her, he ran his fingers lightly down her bare arms until he grabbed her hands. Each hand was pushed behind her back until they touched, and he dragged her tight to his body. She didn't know if it was him who kissed her or if she'd kissed him, but their lips met in a frenzy that always happened when they fought. But this time, no words were spoken in anger, just forgiveness.

CHAPTER TWENTY-FIVE

Harper's alarm woke them at 3 a.m. on Saturday. With a groan, she grabbed her phone and turned off the offending noise. Setting it back onto the nightstand, she snuggled closer to him, and he pulled her closer yet.

"Why are you getting up so early?" he said softly into the darkness.

"Because I have to get the beef tenderloin from the fridge. It needs to rest for two hours and then roast for four." She said lazily.

"At three in the morning?"

"I like to start breakfast to be almost ready at 6 a.m." She wiggled closer to him.

"Three?"

"I maybe left a window for other things."

"How much of a window?" His hand slid up her body and cupped her breast.

She sighed. "Hours."

"We had better use them all up, then," he said and rolled her under him as she giggled.

It was closer to 5 a.m. when he kissed Harper at the door as she walked out, heading for home. She had the day off, and now he knew she had a small wedding she was catering that night. Though she would be home late, she was coming to his house to sleep.

This morning he knew she was getting together with her sisters and mom for breakfast. It was odd how that her stepmom was his missing sister. So far, he hadn't talked to Arabella about finding Seraphina, but he was doing that today in person.

Now that he knew what Harper was doing with her time, it had made it easier for her to be gone. She was just working, and harder than he was. On Thursday, he had ordered pizza for supper, and they had talked about her job, a job she'd had for over three years now. They talked about how she and Lucy were trying to make it work, but since money was low, they both worked second jobs. Harper also explained how she had used the money to remodel their kitchen so they could grow.

She had confessed that she had used his kitchen for weeks without him knowing. Her sisters had been in and out of the house during the day as they helped her, which was how Cliff had been there. He'd picked up Lucy one day.

At her admission, he should have been angry, but she was sitting on the yellow bedspread, naked and eating pizza as she told him. He couldn't be mad at her at that moment. But he did toss the pizza box on the floor and make her apologize, or at least that was what he had planned for her to do.

By midmorning, he was heading to Arabella's house; she had assured him that he was welcome over anytime. Walking up the sidewalk, she opened the door for him, grinning at him as she did.

"Becca says you're in love with Harper."

"Bex doesn't know everything, Arabella." Kaine walked past her into the house. No way was he touching that one.

"But she's right about this one. You love her so much!" Arabella was practically dancing as she spoke.

"Don't get all excited, Arabella. There might be a wrinkle in the love train you're building," he said, picking up Eddie, who had run to him for a hug.

"I think she loves you too, Kaine. I could tell when you were here." Arabella took her son from him.

"Not that. Can we sit? Is Bex here?" He looked around for his personal assistant.

Arabella set her son down and had him run and get his other mom as she led him to the sunroom. It was her favorite room. Sitting down on one of the four chairs in there, he waited for Bex to show up.

"Did she dump you, Kaine? What did you do?" Arabella asked in all seriousness.

"No, she didn't, and I did nothing." If there were something wrong, why would his sister think it was his fault?

"What?" Bex walked into the room, carrying the little boy now. "Kaine messed up a sure thing?"

"Becca, he loves her," Arabella scolded her wife.

"He doesn't. What did you do then?" Bex asked the same thing as Arabella had.

"I didn't do anything," he stated. "Do you remember her mom, Bex?"

"Sera Lovely, her 'not mom,' you mean." Bex sat on Arabella's chair's arm, putting Eddie down as she did.

"Her real name is Seraphina, and she is our sister," he said to his little sister. "She's been in the city the entire time, raising Harper and her sisters, and two of her own.

"*What?*" Arabella looked as shocked as he had been.

"I ran into her at The J on Wednesday night. She was there with her fiancé, who is my lawyer, Harrison," he explained.

"And Harper's mother? How weird was that?" Bex stated, looking right at him.

"Yep. It seemed that she got pregnant, and Mom and Dad disowned her for it. She married a professor, who walked out on her and his kids. She's been raising them on her own ever since."

"Here in the city?" Arabella asked.

"Yes," Kaine said, then pulled out his phone and found the picture of her with Harrison. "Here she is, her and her fiancé."

Both looked, even though Bex should know what they both looked like. But both looked at the sister Arabella hadn't seen in half her life.

"Now that you say you're related, I can see Arabella in her completely. She even acts the same way as you." Bex gave her wife a side hug and kissed the top of her head.

"Does she want to meet me?" Arabella asked.

"Yes, soon. She's going to text me a date. One of her stepdaughters is getting married in a few weeks, and she's busy with that."

"Harper?" Bex asked with a smirk.

"No, Mabel, to Clifton Scott V, whose family is a big deal in this town, and Claudia was dying to meet him. But Harper played her like a fiddle." He grinned at the memory of his ex's face when Harper couldn't remember her last name.

"What does Seraphina say about you dating her stepkid?" Arabella asked.

"Harper said she was pretty okay with it, but she seems pretty laid back about everything with her girls," Kaine explained. Even when they'd talked, she was open about her kids being a little crazy, that they had been since the beginning.

"Wow, a family reunion soon. I'll have to get ready for that." Arabella grinned; she was already ready for it.

CHAPTER TWENTY-SIX

"Harper is banging mom's brother!" Mabel stated in shocked amazement.

The information hadn't gotten out last night, it seemed, but this morning, it was circling the kitchen like a wildfire.

"He's my boss!" she yelled at her younger sister.

"Sorry." Mabel patted her hand gently. "Harper's banging her boss, who is mom's brother!"

Beside Harper, Lucy spit out the piece of muffin she was eating and laughed until tears ran from her eyes. "Banging."

"I am not," Harper tried again.

"Nobody believes you, Harps," Agatha said from her stool. She wasn't laughing, just smirking.

"Stop laughing, everyone. I'm okay with it. They're both adults," Sera chided from the stool she had been sitting at, listening to the entire exchange.

"So, you admit to having a brother?" Buzz asked from the wall she was leaning against in short shorts and a T-shirt that said "Buzzzz."

"Yes, I do. And a sister. Kaine and Arabella. Arabella is the twins' age, and Kaine is mine. We are twins," she said.

"Twins? You have a twin?" Mabel asked her mom in disbelief. Since Sera had never mentioned she was a twin, even as she raised twins.

"Yup. I guess I had to put that part of my life behind me when I was disowned. And then suddenly, I was mother to five, then six and alone. I'm sorry I didn't tell anyone," she said as a tear ran down her cheek.

"It's okay, Mom," Buzz said softly and gave her a big hug.

"I'm going to meet with both of them one day this week. Before the big wedding." She smiled at Mabel, who toasted her with her coffee cup.

"In three weeks," Agatha reminded everyone.

"Two weeks, Agatha," Mabel corrected, as if the short engagement hadn't been the only thing they talked about sometimes.

"But I'm busy in two weeks. I'm free in three," Agatha said with a straight face, making everyone laugh because Agatha never had anything going on.

"So, are you going to keep working for Kaine, Harper? Or are you done this week?" Lucy asked from beside her since she was the most affected if Harper stayed with Kaine.

Harper stiffened at the question. They hadn't talked about it. After today, they only had one full day left together.

"At this point, I haven't been invited to stay," she answered, hoping that they would just drop it. Friday, she had finally hired a cleaning service, and the new chef started on Monday. This time, the chef was willing to work around Kaine's schedule.

"Do you want to stay?" Sera asked.

"I don't know what I want. Now, can we just drop it? I don't want to talk about it!" Harper tossed the pan on the counter.

"With that, I am heading out. I'm hoping to catch Cliff before he gets out of bed," Mabel said with a wink. Her fiancé was in her bed this morning. It was why Buzz hadn't claimed it yet.

"Gross. I do not need that image in my brain. I'm going to shower to wash it out." Buzz followed her sister out of the room.

"I'm going to bed," Agatha said, staring at Harper as she left.

"And that means Harper is a buzzkill," Lucy added, putting the leftovers in plastic containers.

"Sorry, I just don't need my life talked about by everyone," Harper argued at the remaining members of the family.

"Then don't have a life, Harps, or else we'll talk about it," Sera said to her. Personal lives and professional lives had always been discussed amongst each other. Nothing had ever been off-limits.

"I don't have a life. I work all the time!" she replied, pointing to the bowl she was currently mixing in.

"Keep telling yourself that, sweetheart. It's Lucy that doesn't get any time off these days. Your second job doesn't seem to involve much work."

"What are you saying?" Harper demanded, but she felt heat rising at her mom's words.

"Just that you may not have it as bad as others in this house. That maybe you are enjoying your time with Kaine, and that it hasn't been a job in weeks," Sera said and spun off her chair.

Watching her mom walk out of the room, Harper knew she was right. No longer did she think about leaving to go to his house as going to work; it was going home now. Being with him was where she wanted to end the day, and she missed him when she didn't end it in his bed. It wasn't even just the sex anymore; it was him.

"I'm not overworked, Harper." Lucy's words made her turn to her sister, whose eyes had deep shadows under them. When had that happened? Harper hadn't even noticed them before.

"When did you get up this morning?" Harper asked, thinking about her alarm going off at 3 a.m.

"It doesn't matter." Lucy turned to reach into the fridge to grab something.

Without thinking, Harper slammed the fridge door closed on her sister, leaving the other woman looking at the closed door in anger. "What was that for?"

"What time did you get up this morning?" She asked again.

Lucy looked at her feet. "Noon."

"It's eight in the morning!"

"I had the Kimball party last night, which lasted until close to 1 a.m., and then I went to the offices and cleaned to get that out of the way. Then you were here when I got out of the shower." Her little sister shrugged as if it was no big deal that she had worked for over eighteen hours straight.

"I helped prep that," Harper stated, seeing now that it hadn't been enough, that she had relied on her sister too much for weeks.

"You did, and Agatha helped serve, but most of it was on me. And I nailed it!" Lucy said happily, moving away from all the work she had actually done.

"How often have you been doing that? I know your cleaning is at night. How many nights have you not slept because of me?"

"Maybe three," he shrugged again.

"Only three?" Harper said in relief.

"Three a week. You do a lot, Harper. When you are not here, I have to do a lot more," Lucy replied, leaning back into the island.

"Go to bed, Lucy. I will take care of this. You'll pass out if you don't sleep." Harper pushed her away from the food.

"I'm okay so far. I can sleep tomorrow," Lucy said, shaking her hands off.

Harper gave her a flat look. "Yes, you can. But you are off today, the entire day,"

"But there's too much to do." Lucy looked around the kitchen. They hadn't even started getting ready for the wedding yet.

"Go to bed and don't think about it. I'll call someone else if I need help. You need time off." Harper momentarily saw the relief in Lucy's eyes, but then it was gone, and she just looked tired.

"I'll come back when I wake up," Lucy said in defeat.

Watching her walk out of the room, Harper realized she had left everything for Lucy to handle on her own. Lucy had another job that wasn't sleeping with her boss. It was hard work cleaning office buildings. Then she'd added almost running the catering by herself all month to her list.

Two nights a week helping her had not been enough. Harper may have been the one with the new job, but it had been Lucy doing all the work.

CHAPTER TWENTY-SEVEN

HARPER CAME HOME early Sunday morning and had crashed, like the first day she had been there. Also like the first day, they had woken early and had sex. But they had stayed in bed most of the rest of day, only leaving for meals and to watch a movie in the evening.

This morning he had gotten up and made it to the office at just after 6 a.m., and it felt good to be that early. So far, Harper hadn't told him what days she needed off, and he hadn't asked because she always told him when she wasn't going to be there in the evening. And lately, she slept at the house on her days off anyway.

At 10 a.m., he got a text from her. All it said was "bye." She had never texted that she was leaving his house before. She also sent an email that detailed information about the new chef she'd hired. The woman seemed interesting and not a French chef at all, but she was willing to cook French food most of the time. Kaine was excited to get home and see if Harper was actually going to eat the woman's food or not. He really doubted it.

The rest of the email was about a cleaning service she had hired that was going to come twice a week and would also clean at Arabella's twice a week for three months, which had made Kaine smile that

Harper was thinking of his sister and how she was going to manage when she had to babies at her house.

"Morning, Kaine," Bex said as she came in. He hadn't seen her this morning at all.

"Hey, Bex. Did you take time off this morning?" he asked.

"Yes, I always take time off on the first Monday of the month. Doctors appointment for Bella."

"I forgot."

"Last time I did, you hired yourself a woman. Did you do that again? Your personal assistant seems to be here today." Bex laughed.

"Haha," he said sarcastically.

"Did you extend your contract then? Or is it over?" Bex tossed her phone on his desk as she did when they were talking about personal stuff.

"It's not like that," he stated, realizing the contract was up today. They hadn't talked about it, and he had no idea what they were doing now.

"You mean you let the contract expire and forgot to tell her you were in fucking love with her?" Bex demanded, angrier than he had expected of her.

"I don't love her!" he said to her again.

"Well then, good thing she's gone. Are you going to find another sex buddy? I would like to see you with less of an annoying person. Maybe this new personal assistant." Bex pointed behind her, and Kaine was glad she had shut the door on her way in.

"No, Bex. I am not," he said with anger, as if he could just move on to another woman.

"Maybe you can just start going to bars like normal a man and pick up a hot number when you need one? Or there are services for that. I don't know of any, but I assume." Bex shrugged.

"Did you just compare Harper to a hooker?" he seethed.

"It was just sex, wasn't it, Kaine? No emotions—the perfect woman!" she fed him back his words. "Or did she turn into the perfect woman, and you let your emotions get involved?"

"I am not talking about my love life with you." He folded his arms.

"Love life? That seems to be an appropriate name for it. Or it was until you let her leave."

"I don't have time for a love life." He sighed. Sixteen-hour days didn't make for a good relationship after all.

"You were getting to the right mix in the end, coming in after 7 a.m. and leaving around 6 p.m. Eat meals with her and relax in the evening. Not working nonstop and ignoring her until she's fucking someone else. Or don't you actually remember what happened to your marriage?" Bex said.

"Really? You're bringing that up?" he demanded. He was well aware of how that had ended. The worst part was that Bex was right; he had been the problem, just like with Harper.

Except Claudia wasn't like Harper at all. Claudia had never had a career of her own, no ambition beyond being married to a successful man. In the month Harper had been living with him, she had dedicated every other hour of the day to her business. Before that, she had found a way to have a second job that left her entire focus on her main job. What he saw as lack of ambition was just a lack of dedication towards a job she didn't like. Her entire focus was on her first job: her own business.

Bex continued to lecture him. "I told you before, Kaine. You have to make time for a woman. Any woman. And if you want this woman, you will have to start now."

"So, who do you think will do all the work I do if I'm not here?"

"Well, you have employees who could use more work, and I think they could do it too. Even if you don't."

"I just like to know it gets done."

"You have so many people in this building who want the same thing and have the training to do the same thing, but you've never let them do it. You have people underutilized, just waiting for a moment to shine." Bex jumped to her feet and started to pace around the room.

"Name one," he demanded sharply.

"*Me.*" She stopped and pointed at herself.

"I thought you were happy working for me?" he asked in surprise. She had never said otherwise. Not once.

"I have always loved working for you. When I started here, I didn't plan to be your personal assistant for long. And I never thought about moving up to your executive assistant. That wasn't the path I wanted, but you did, and I was honored to be here beside you." Bex folded her arms as she talked.

"What was your plan?"

"I have a degree in marketing, Kaine. I have always wanted to do that on some level." Bex sat down on the edge of her seat, as if she would bolt if he said the wrong thing.

"You never said anything."

"Because you don't listen to me. You only listen to yourself," she reminded him.

"I do listen to you."

"Then delegate! Find the right people. Become a normal person. You now have a girlfriend, or you could just marry the girl. Have kids and have a life. Most people do it; I think you can too. Your sister wants nieces and nephews. We can't have all the kids in this family. I mean, we will if we have to, but ..." Bex grinned at him.

Ignoring her innuendo about her and his sister's sex life, he told her the truth, the reason he hadn't brought up the end of the contract with Harper. "I don't know if she wants all of that with me."

"Maybe you should talk to her. I mean, I don't want to talk to her, but you can."

"You do know if we do get together, you'll have to spend holidays with her," he reminded his assistant, who might just be warming to the idea of Harper being around.

"I am well aware, but then again, she is your sister's kid, so maybe she would be there anyway. And Arabella and Sera are really enjoying the entire big family thing. Holidays are going to be changing," Bex replied, which meant that the sisters had gotten in touch while he was spending the weekend with Harper.

"I ..." He didn't even know what to say. Seeing Harper at family functions was going to kill him, especially when she started dating someone else.

"Just call her, Kaine. You might find out she feels the same way."

"And if she doesn't?"

"Let me rephrase that. Kaine, she loves you also. Call her, text her, or go to her. Just don't let her go."

"Is my sister rubbing off on you?"

"Kaine Hawthorn, what you feel for this woman is exactly how I feel for Bella. Back then, I thought I could ignore her and forget her, but I couldn't. Love isn't like that for us." She picked up her phone and pointed it at him.

"I let Claudia go," he reminded her. She had been with him when it had happened. Though back then, she hadn't been as candid with him as she was now.

"You didn't love her like you love Harper, and you know I'm right. You didn't know what love was until you found it with the right person."

"What if she realizes that I'm not what she wants? How did you get over that?" He laid it out for her. This woman made him vulnerable in ways his wife never had.

Bex smiled at his questions. "I'll tell you the moment it happens. Your sister is the most amazing person I know and will ever know. What she sees in me is a mystery that I am not going to solve, and I hope she doesn't either."

"I have to figure it out," he said more to himself than to Bex.

She shook her head and looked at her phone again. "I'm taking the rest of the day off."

"It's not even noon." He looked at the clock on the wall just to make sure.

"I have a wife who needs to know how much I love her." Bex winked and walked out, not even waiting for approval. She didn't need it.

CHAPTER TWENTY-EIGHT

"Bank security guard, overnight. Hours are good, and the pay is excellent." Harper pointed to the ad in the paper. Buzz had brought it home the day before because her article was supposed to be in it but hadn't been. "I think I could do that."

"You can stop a bank robbery? You?" Lucy asked as she measured out flour for the cake they were making. It was a wedding cake for Maby, and if it turned out well, they were freezing it for the week until the wedding. If not, they had to start again until it was perfect. Maybe they should have worked on this earlier.

"I'm pretty tough when I want to be." Harper flexed her muscles. No way did they make the gray "Grand Cannon" T-shirt stretch, but they were there.

"You are not, and you would have to carry a gun. Do you even own a gun?" Lucy dumped another cup of flour in the bowl, causing a cloud of flour to waft up into the air.

"I think they have the guns there, Lucy. It's not a 'bring your own gun' job."

"I think they want you to know how to use a gun at least. And I think if you're willing to shoot at someone, you should have at least

shot one once in your life. Or held one … or seen one in person."
Another cup went in.

"Moving on." Harper went back to reading the paper.

"I think you should just crawl back to your boss and keep that job.
It was a good one—no guns or training needed." Lucy put the flour
aside and grabbed the sugar.

"No, he didn't want to extend the contract, and you were working
too hard." Harper looked at her sister. The bags under her eyes had
faded a little since she was home to make sure her sister went to bed
every night. Making sure her sister slept was easier than making sure
she herself slept. She hadn't done much since leaving Kaine's house.
Add to that the weekend, and she was tired, just not enough to sleep.

"I was fine. I was getting used to it. Also, I was thinking that if you
went back, I could quit my job," Lucy said, not looking at Harper as
she poured sugar into a separate bowl.

"We either both work, or we both don't," Harper replied. It was
what they had decided from the beginning. Though she did think Lucy
should get a different job, a better job with better hours.

"Okay, sign me up for sex with my boss as my job, and I'll work forever.
You know, as long as he knows what he's doing." Lucy laughed at herself.

"I was not having sex with my boss!" Harper threw the paper at
her sister.

"You were too!" Lucy dodged it, though the paper didn't fly far
enough to actually hit her. "Hey, I would if it had been me. Hot!"

"Shut up!" Harper started around the island.

"Hot uncle sex!" Lucy laughed, running from the kitchen, knowing
what Harper was planning.

"*Shut up!*" Harper was chasing her up the stairs to the second floor.

"Kaine and Harper, sitting in a tree!" Lucy sang as she headed up
another flight of stairs.

"F-U-C-K-I-N-G!" Agatha joined in. She was sitting at her easel as
Harper came into her room. "First comes—" Harper took her down
before she could say another word. Lucy had been too far away.

"Shut up, you two!" Harper yelled.

Agatha was instantly off balance as her chair crashed to the ground, and Agatha ended up under her sister. Sitting on Agatha, Harper threw anything she could get her hands on at Lucy, who was heading back for the stairs. First pencils and pens, then she grabbed a leg of Agatha's easel, tipping it and sending papers everywhere in the room.

That gave Agatha the strength to roll her off and onto the floor with a thud. Jumping to her feet, she grabbed Harper by the leg and dragged her towards the stairs, through the mess she had created. Harper was using her loose leg to get away from her before the woman actually pulled her down the stairs—it wasn't working.

"*Stop!*" Sera yelled at the top of her lungs.

Thankfully, Agatha did, but then she turned and kicked Harper in the side, hard. "Do not bring your fights into my room. Ever!"

"It was Lucy!" Harper defended herself, but she hadn't seen Agatha this mad in years. Her baggy sweatshirt and leggings were the same as she had worn the day before, and her hair was in a uniquely Agatha cut, but it was a mess. Maybe she needed to make sure this sister was getting sleep also, but at least she was eating now.

"I don't fucking care!" Agatha yelled and kicked her one more time and left her room, walking past Sera on the way. Neither acknowledged the other in passing. Lucy was gone from the room already.

"Feeling better?" Sera asked her. Anger was etched onto her face.

"No, it was Lucy! She started it." She tried the same excuse as she rubbed her side. There was going to be a bruise.

"No, you tipped over Agatha's work. She doesn't get in the way of your work. In fact, she's even willing to help you." Reminding her of all the times Agatha hadn't wanted to help with catering but always showed up. Grumpy and grumbling, but there.

"I didn't mean to, Sera." Harper sat up but was still sitting on the floor. "We were just fighting, and it got away from us. You know how it is."

"I heard the fight, but you need to leave everyone else out of it." Sera turned and headed down the stairs.

"Sorry I messed with your favorite, Mom!" Harper yelled at her.

Everyone knew, but nobody brought it up: Agatha was her mom's favorite. Had been for years.

To her surprise, Sera came back up the stairs. "You know what, Harper? She's my favorite because she needs to be. The rest of you four have the outside world to tell you that you're special and that you're something. Away from here, she has never had the confidence of a Lovely. Agatha isn't like everyone else, so I baby her a little. You being in a shitty mood and hurting her feelings doesn't help that."

"I'm not in a shitty mood!"

"Really?" Sera gave her a look that dared Harper to lie to her.

"What are you saying?"

"That you maybe need to go back to 'work,'" her mom said, using air quotes around the word work, telling Harper everyone knew her job had been a sham.

"Fuck you and this entire family!" she yelled at her retreating form, knowing her mom was right; her mood was sour. But she didn't know how to change it on her own.

"I'm torn between being hurt by your words and saying you already fucked part of her family," Buzz said while coming up the stairs, her red hair a mess still from sleep.

"Be hurt!" Harper yelled at her, already in a fighting mood. What was another battle after the last few? Why not have everyone in the house pissed at her?

"I am more amused still by you actually fucking Mom's brother. Twin brother. Was it like she was there?" The redhead was smirking as she made it completely up the stairs. She was still in her pink pajama shorts and light green T-shirt that said "Buzzzz" on it.

"Gross!"

"It is. Do you want help fixing her easel?" Buzz pointed to the mess.

"Yes, she's pissed at me and maybe Lucy, but mostly me," Harper admitted.

"I don't think she had slept yet, so she was extra crabby." Buzz started gathering up pencils off the stairway landing.

"Crabby, but healthy-looking. Last year at this time, I broke her arm. It just snapped. Just skin and bones." Harper gave a shake at the memory; it had happened too fast and easily. She hadn't even been trying to hurt her, just twist her arm behind her back. Nothing more than she had done before, many times.

Harper picked up the chair and set it on its wheels, realizing what a mess she had made of her sister's work. Nearly as much as she had made of her own life.

"I think she has put on thirty pounds since then. She's looking good," Buzz agreed. "Have you even talked to the ass since you left?"

"No, the month was over. I guess he didn't feel what I felt," Harper admitted. She had feelings for the man, but he hadn't returned them. Though she had known from the beginning that he didn't have feelings for her, she had wanted them in the end.

"I think he did. Did you ever talk about it? About anything?"

"Yes and no. Mostly no."

"Just send him a 'thinking of you' text." Buzz lifted the table that was on its side.

"I am not thinking of him." Harper helped, getting it back into position.

"Yes, you are. You are so in fucking love with the ass, you don't know what to do with yourself. And you're taking it out on everyone." Buzz started picking up papers and setting them haphazardly on the desk.

"That I can assure you I am not. No way am I in love with him. A bit of like, that's all," Harper lied. No need for Buzz to know the truth.

"Keep telling yourself that, Harps. One day, maybe you will even believe it," Buzz said as she picked up the last of the pencils and set them on Agatha's chair. None of the sisters actually knew how Agatha liked her art stuff set up. She liked to be alone when she worked.

Harper knew Buzz was right; she was in love with Kaine, but he wasn't ever going to love her back. He had gotten what he wanted, and he didn't want it anymore.

It had been an emotionless arrangement. It was her fault she had gotten emotional about it.

CHAPTER TWENTY-NINE

When Kaine got home from work Wednesday night, Harper wasn't there. It was day three, and he still wasn't used to her not being there. The chef was also gone when he got home, mostly because he had all but told her he wasn't going to be home before 9 p.m. that week. His house was completely empty.

Tossing the mail on the kitchen counter, he was surprised to see nothing was in the oven. Nothing was in the fridge. On the stove was a note from the chef.

Reading through it, he realized that Harper had put a clause in the woman's contract. If he didn't make it home at a decent time for three days, she was let go. And now his chef was gone. Nobody would be making his meals—no Harper, no chef, nobody.

It wasn't even because he wanted to work late; he just wanted to avoid his house without Harper in it. With her not rushing in at just before seven, there was no need to even be here. The house was silent without her.

But so far, he hadn't heard anything from her—no texts or calls. Nor had he contacted her. At this point, he had no idea what to say to her.

Yes, he wanted her in his life, but what if she didn't feel the same?

What if she had only been there because it was her job, and now that it was over, she was relieved to be done with him?

It was that thought that had him trying to keep busy enough so that he didn't have enough time in the day to contact her. He didn't want to have a spare minute to reach out to her only to have her reject him.

To his relief, Bex hadn't said another word about Harper since Monday, and not just because she was too busy trying to find a few key people to take over some aspects of his job. Within an hour of her leaving on Monday, he knew she was right, and he also knew she deserved to not simply be his executive assistant anymore. She wouldn't be his first promotion, but he was sure it was going to be his most important.

Flipping through his mail, he saw a gold envelope with the return address of C Scott V on it. Quickly opening it, he was it was an invitation to Cliff and Mabel's wedding. A wedding happening on Saturday. The invitation that Claudia had been dreaming of was in his hand. He couldn't imagine what she would say if she ever found out that his sister was the mother of the bride for the wedding she so wanted to go to.

Cliff's words from the party rang in his ear, "When you find a Lovely lady, you get her off the market as soon as possible." And the man was doing that. He was lucky enough to have locked his woman down.

Looking at the invitation again, he wondered if it had been sent by Cliff and Mabel or Sera. Either was a possibility. The only one who hadn't sent it was Harper … because they were done.

After tossing the invitation on the table, he went to bed and hoped he'd be able to sleep that night—something that had been elusive since Harper wasn't in his bed with him. Sleep or not, he knew he would be up early to go back to work, even if work wasn't the same without her to come home to.

Yesterday he had lunch with Sera and Arabella for the first time in two decades. It was surreal that they had been in the same town for years, and none of them had realized it. It was also mind-blowing how much the sisters were alike in mannerisms and looks. Sera had either been very excepting of Arabella being married to a woman or could fake it.

The sisters had shared pictures of their children and spouses, or soon to be spouses, something that Kaine couldn't share with them. Though he had caught a glimpse or two of Harper in the photos, one from her teen years with one of the brunettes, one was obviously taken in France with a guy, and one with the little girl he had thought was her daughter.

Not that either of his sisters had said anything about Harper, but both had her on their minds. He knew it because Arabella kept giving him looks, and Sera was a bit more standoffish with him that day than at the party the other night. They were not sharing with him because of Harper.

Picking up the invite one more time, he realized that he knew where she was going to be. For one day, he could see her, talk to her, and find out if she wanted to be with him even if she had no contract requiring her to be there. He had to know.

He wasn't going to spend the rest of his life wondering if taking one step would have been enough. Maybe they were both too scared to take that first step. They may both be the boss, but neither were good at taking directions from anyone, even themselves.

CHAPTER THIRTY

FOR THE LAST THREE HOURS, Harper had been really regretting saying she would be happy to be in Maby and Cliff's wedding party. Sure, at the time, she thought it would be great fun but walking down the aisle with a man named Chester wasn't her idea of fun. Cliff's step-cousin was already drunk, and it was mid-afternoon.

"Smile, Harps." Lucy grinned at her. She had been pared with Cliff's actual cousin, Blake, who was tall, dark, and handsome, and fully sober.

"I should have said no," Harper whispered at her sister, but it echoed through the cathedral. Mabel had buckled to pressure from Sera to marry in the same place Sera was going to get married in a few months' time. Mabel didn't care where she married her man, just that it happened, and fast. Which Harper had attributed to her sister wanting to get Sera off her back, but was starting to think her sister really just wanted to be married to the former party animal.

"Too late," whispered Mabel, earning her a scowl from the priest. They weren't even catholic. How Sera made that happen would never be known.

Rolling her eyes at her little sister in her gorgeous white gown, she couldn't believe the wedding was already here. Not that the engagement was long since they had been dating officially for around a month, but the dates were hazy, and the couple wasn't actually telling anyone what they were. Still, Maby was the first of the group to get married, not counting Sera's marriage to their dad, which nobody actually counted.

Though Sera had pretended to be upset Maby was getting to the alter first, she really wasn't. At this point in her wedding preparations, Sera was willing to let everyone get married because she had so many plans, she needed to share them. This particular wedding was going to have doves released at the end, something that Harrison had said no to for their own wedding. It seemed only Harrison could say no to Sera.

On top of that, the entire church was completely full. It seemed her new brother-in-law wasn't just a fun party guy, but someone everyone wanted to see get married. Kaine's ex wasn't the only one coveting an invitation, but she was maybe the only one in the city not actually here. Or maybe she was there; Harper couldn't see from one face to the next.

"Do you think anyone in here actually wants to be here?" she whispered to Lucy, trying to be quieter this time.

"Nope, even the bride and groom are only doing the wedding for the honeymoon." Lucy chuckled. She, of course, would know. It was her twin and her best friend. But then again, Harper knew too. Maby and Cliff didn't hide the fact that they were attracted to each other. A lot. "And of course, Sera," she added.

Harper gave Lucy a warning look. "Do not tell her that they were married this morning at their house. She will be so pissed."

"Cliff is nothing but a showman," she agreed.

This morning, she had gotten a text at 1 a.m. They all had but Sera, who was at Harrison's with the little two. It had been an SOS from the bride, who was staying with the groom against her mother's best judgment.

They had all hurried over, wondering what could possibly make Maby not want to marry Cliff. Nobody had even changed from their pajamas. When they got there, Cliff had an officiant there, and he was going to marry Mabel in front of her four sisters and nobody else—just like she had wanted when he had first proposed. Okay, maybe it was more on a beach than in the living room, but she could bend her expectations if needed. Mabel had wanted Sera and the girls there, but Sera would blow a gasket at the entire thing. Then the daytime wedding wouldn't be needed, so they were doing all this for her.

Now here they were, in front of hundreds at a sham wedding because the couple had been married for over twelve hours and were sure to have consummated that union as soon as the sisters left hours before. Maby had even been wearing the wedding ring all day, and Sera hadn't seemed to notice.

But they pretended for Mom, and Harper hoped she was enjoying it. Based on the piles of tissues and the huge smile, she was. It was like the best day of her life. The woman was going to be a puddle on her big day, and she only had around a month to wait now.

All morning had been spent getting ready for the big day; from hair to makeup, they had the royal treatment. And all to make her baby sister into Mrs. Clifton Scott V, but it was worth it.

As the priest announced them married, Harper heard her new brother-in-law say, "Finally," and he kissed his bride until Harper was sure that they weren't actually going to stop. Over the last month, she had been privy to their make-out sessions, and they didn't ever end without outside intervention.

Then, to everyone's surprise, or at least everyone who didn't know him well, he picked up his bride and carried her out of the church. Maby tossed her bouquet at the audience as she laughed at her new husband's antics. Sera only shook her head at the couple—it was a total Cliff move.

Harper plastered a smile on her face and headed down the aisle behind Lucy and Blake, with Chester on her arm. She was just happy he didn't think he should carry her anywhere. He was sure to drop her, and she would have to murder him; heck, if he touched her, he would have to die.

Just as she pushed him away from her—because she was sure he touched her ass—she saw Arabella in the audience. She was holding

Eddy, and Bex had her arm around her. But on the other side of Bex was Kaine, all gorgeous and sexy and handsome. All here.

Chester grabbed her arm and pulled her away from her view of Kaine's blue eyes, though she wasn't actually close enough to see them. She knew that they were there; she had missed them.

"Do you think Cliff will remember he has to go to the reception?" Lucy asked, her eyes on her best friend still carrying his bride right out the church doors and into the sunshine.

"Maby will make him."

"He's having sex with her before, though." Lucy scrunched up her nose at the thought.

"Yes, he is, and I think it's her idea." Harper grabbed Lucy into a hug. Their sister was a married woman now.

"Where are Maby and Cliff?" Sera demanded behind them, tears all but gone.

"Already gone. They decided against the greeting line," Lucy said, knowing Sera was going to be mad after all her planning.

Harrison came up behind her and wrapped his arms around her. "It's their wedding, Sera. Let it go."

"But they should greet their guests." Sera's eyes were starting to well up with tears.

"Remember, they don't know most of those people. We'll greet our guests at our wedding." He kissed her neck as Buzz and Agatha came out of the church with Emma and Violet.

"Promise?" she whispered.

"Promise. We are going to have the most beautiful wedding." He kissed her again.

"I know. This was just a dry run. I see some areas for improvement." Sera wasn't even going to pretend she hadn't put this entire wedding on as a practice run for her own.

"Of course, you do." Harrison winked at his future stepdaughters, who were always judging how he was treating the woman. Always.

"Can we just go to the reception then?" Agatha asked, not wanting to stick around. Today she was in a dress like she'd promised, though Harper was pretty sure Sera would have rather seen her in jeans and a

"Grand Cannon" T-shirt than the baggy blue dress that did nothing but hide her figure from the world. It was more of a tent than a dress, and she had pared it with matching tennis shoes. The color was spot on. The look was not.

Sera hadn't commented on it yet and probably wouldn't. Everyone liked that she was no longer skin and bones; everyone but Agatha, who was uncomfortable with it. Her dress today proved it.

"Okay, everyone can go to the reception. Harrison and I will work the crowd here." Sera made a plan, letting all the girls get away.

Harper wanted to linger, to see Kaine again since he probably wouldn't make it to the reception. Though Sera was his sister, he most likely wanted to avoid Harper … because he was done with her.

Since it was a Scott wedding, they rode to the reception in limos. All the sisters squeezed into one, with Violet on Buzz's lap, and Lucy practically on Harper's.

Lucy leaned over to her and whispered, "The ass was there. Is he going to the reception?"

"He was there because he and Sera are related. I don't know if he's going to the reception or not."

"He is," Buzz said from across the car. "I saw him eye fuck you during the ceremony. He'll be there."

"Buzz, language. Sera said no more swearing in front of the kids," Lucy scolded their little sister.

"I think that they already know *the* word. Their mother said it this morning, and they were both there," Buzz complained.

"I've never seen that happen, but maybe soon," Emma stated, her eyes on her phone.

"It's very rare. You should put it out of your mind," Agatha added, always a little more protective of Sera's babies.

"Maybe if uncle Kaine comes to the reception, I will see it." Emma shrugged.

"One can always hope that uncle Kaine comes at the reception." Lucy chuckled and nudged her.

"She needs it," Agatha said under her breath and glanced at Violet, who was looking at Buzz's phone now.

"That she does," Emma agreed with a smirk. She knew what they were talking about.

"Thank you, everyone. Always nice to feel loved," Harper bit out sarcastically.

"That is all we hope for you, Harps." Lucy laughed again as the car came to a stop in front of Pembroke house, the reception spot of choice for Sera. How she had secured it in less than a month, Harper would never know, but something most likely got the boot so they could be there today.

Once out of the car, she and Lucy headed to the kitchen. They wouldn't let anyone else cater the event. Since they had found a ton of wait staff, no sisters would be working it. Unless something went awry, and then all hands would be on deck—even the bride and groom.

Busying herself, Harper tried to force Kaine from her mind. She didn't want to be excited about him maybe coming to the reception. She couldn't let her hopes raise too much in case he didn't. After all, he could just be there to see his niece get married, nothing else.

CHAPTER THIRTY-ONE

"SHE'S ALREADY AT THE RECEPTION," Sera said to Kaine as he looked around the entry area of the church for Harper's silver dress, the one he had pictured taking off of her for the entire hour of the wedding. All the while, her back was to him, showing off a zipper that was begging him to open it.

He was glad he came, not just because he had gotten another look at the woman he was willing to admit he had fallen for, but because he had learned more about where she came from today.

For instance, he had learned that no matter what, Sera was her mother. She was listed as the mother of the bride, and no other parents were listed for her, nor were any mentioned as having passed. Harper had once told him that Lucy was Cliff's friend, and Lucy was listed as the twin of the bride and the very best friend of the groom. Harper herself had been listed as the big bossy sister of the bride. Though only two stood up there, the two other sisters in the audience weren't hard to pick out. The redhead kept looking at him, daring him to do something.

Seeing Sera and Harrison holding hands as they came in, he could tell they were very much in love. And he had seen his nieces, the real ones, and knew they were also well-loved. Not just by their parents, but by the sisters that lived with them.

Arabella had whispered to him that all the girls still lived at home and that Sera was finding it hard to leave them behind, but Harrison was in no way moving in with five adult women. In fact, Mabel was still an official resident of the house, even today. Then his sister said something about bedrooms and fighting. It seemed the family was very close.

"What?" he turned to Sera. It was still a surprise to see his twin, even if it was her daughter's wedding.

"Harper. I sent all the girls to the reception. She's as lost as you are," Sera pointed out.

"I don't know what you are talking about," he replied. She didn't know how he felt. They were basically strangers, after all.

"I'm sure you don't. My kids aren't as perfect as I always see them, Kaine. Harper may be bossy as hell, but her heart has always been fragile. She's the one who hurt the most when Judith left. I think they were closer than Harper has ever let on. Since then, she hasn't let people close. I shouldn't have let her go to France alone when she was so young. But I was young then also, and I couldn't see that she was just getting away before the others left home, to be gone before she could be left again. She always tries be ahead of the pain, but it catches her anyway."

"She's pretty confident and put-together."

"No, she is bossy and opinionated and pushy. She needs a man who can put up with that and stick by her side to *make* her feel confident and put-together. But also, one who can put her in her place and not let her steamroll over everyone and everything. I think you two would be good together if you both could just get over being the one who is right for once." Sera smiled.

"We are very different people," he said. It had been that way from the beginning.

"No, Kaine, you are almost too similar to get along. You both are over-achieving workaholics who can't sit still for a few minutes at a time, but you both need to stop and look around every once in a while. Breathe."

"That didn't happen in the month we were together."

"Of course, it did. You both stopped working so late to be together. Maybe you can work in vacations. If you love her enough, you will make it happen. She might just do the same."

"I don't love her."

"Just as much as she doesn't love you. So similar, it is scary." Sera squeezed his arm and walked away.

As with coming to the wedding, he rode with Bex and Arabella and Eddie in Arabella's van to the reception. Yes, he should have driven, but Arabella said she would, so he let her.

Bex shot him looks from the passenger seat, looks that said she hated that van also. But she loved the woman who loved the van, so there she was, making her wife happy. Her eyes told him that he needed to love Harper for who she was, not who he wanted her to be.

Once in the hall, he was amazed again by how many people were already there. The place was nearly packed. With a smile, he didn't even look around for Harper. He knew where she would be: the kitchen.

On his way, he passed Lucy, who was wearing silver and not white, and Buzz, who was laughing with some guy at a table. But she winked at him. Did that mean she didn't hate him anymore? You never knew what was coming from the redhead.

Pushing through the door of the kitchen, he saw her immediately, still in silver with her hair up. She was pulling something from the oven, her hands encased in oven mitts.

"Reception is out there," she said, barely looking up from what she was doing.

"I know. I wanted to see you." Her movements instantly stopped at his words. "Your harp is gone," he added.

Slowly, she set the pan on the counter, tossing the oven mitts as she did it. "Maby said no, so Lucy made it disappear."

"I missed it." Moving towards her, she didn't move. Her eyes saw only him, just as his saw only her.

"It's not Scott wedding-appropriate, or so the bride said," she continued, her hand reaching back to touch the spot.

"I missed it before the wedding. I missed it all week."

She breathed deeply. "Contract was over."

"The contract was null and void weeks ago. My emotions were involved from day one. From missing you the moment you left me to jealousy of those who got to be with you when I couldn't. And I couldn't ask you what you were doing." He walked to her and was happy when she didn't move away from him.

"I'm busy … always busy." She shrugged, causing the dress to shimmer in the bright lights.

"I was too, but we both have to take a look at our lives and make time for each other. As long as you want there to be an 'each other.'" He finally was close enough to touch her, so he ran a finger down her arm.

"That's not going to be easy. You love to work. You prefer sixteen-hour days every day. I don't want to be waiting for you to find time for me. Then one day stop making time for me." She whispered the last.

"Bex said I have to learn to delegate, and so do you. We can help each other."

"Always Bex." The half-smile she gave, he had to kiss.

Instantly, she responded, and he couldn't get enough of her. She tasted of nothing but pure Harper. He ran his hands down her side until he could pull her closer to him, tight against his body.

"Harps, Cliff said the party is continuing at the house," a voice said from behind them.

With a groan, she ended the kiss and looked over his shoulder. "The meal isn't even served."

"Let me rephrase that. Stop sucking face with the ass, and let's get out of here." He knew it was the redhead before he even turned around. So much for her not hating him.

"Food for three hundred, Buzz," Harper stated, not leaving his arms, not looking away from him.

"And staff to manage it. Limos are leaving in ten." Today the redhead was in black from head to toe, or not actually head, and it didn't get even close to her toes. The dress fit like it was made for her, and it probably was. The shoes were as skimpy as the dress, and he had no idea how she kept it on.

"*Delegate.*" He kissed Harper's ear as he said it, seeing the indecision in her eyes.

"Easy for you to say," Harper whispered back to him.

"Ass, just grab her and meet at the limo in ten. It might be tight," Buzz mumbled as she spun on her heels and left the kitchen, presumably to look for more sisters.

"She still doesn't like me." He couldn't stop touching her.

"Maybe you can win her over one day."

"Are you going to let me go to your house so I can start making your sisters like me?" he begged. He wasn't above begging this woman for anything.

"If you want to. It is nothing like your house, though."

"I want to see where you spend your days. Maybe I can stop any fights that might happen, prevent a few black eyes." He ran his finger over her eye that had long since healed.

"Good luck."

It only took ten minutes in a limo with all four sisters and Cliff to make Kaine see he was never going to stop the fighting. From most of them calling him "ass" and two objecting to him being in the same limo as them to Harper yelling at them both until the groom shoved them both into the car against their wills.

The argument was still raging when beside him, Lucy got a call on her phone. With a single look, she had the entire car silent. "Hey, Sera."

From his spot, he could hear his sister questioning Lucy where she was and if she knew where everyone else was. Lucy lied through her teeth and stated she was in the bathroom and had no idea where anyone else was. Then she spent a few more minutes insisting it was not something she ate.

Hanging up the phone, Buzz stated loudly, "Mom is going to kill you for lying to her."

"The bride made me do it." Lucy pointed to her.

"I did no such thing." The bride protested just as loudly.

"Now, Lucy, you cannot besmirch my lovely wife's name." Cliff shifted the woman onto his lap, which caused the bride to giggle.

"You're an ass too. What is it with women in this family and their attraction to asses?" Buzz stated as her phone went off. Everyone knew from her expression who it was.

One by one, they all got the call, and they all lied to their mother. Until the black-haired one spilled the beans. He could hear his sister yelling from across the car as Agatha hung up on her.

"As if she would never know. Everyone was gone!" she defended herself.

"I'm taking a vote on kicking Agatha out of the family," Lucy stated, but only Lucy and Buzz's hands went in the air.

"Outnumbered, Lucy Maud. I stay," Agatha said smugly as the car stopped in front of a large old house with every light on.

"I would take you down if I wasn't in my pretty dress," Lucy stated, running her hands down her body.

"I really like it," Kaine commented, though it wasn't hers he necessarily liked.

"Gross man, she's your niece." Buzz lightly slapped the back of his head as she exited the car after the bride and groom.

"Not really," he argued, though it was true.

"Yeah, really. Uncle Ass." Agatha pushed past him to get out of the car first.

Taking Harper's hand, they walked slowly into the house because outside, they had a moment to themselves. Once inside the house, everyone was gone, they had all headed up the stairs. The only evidence that they were there were heels left by the door in a haphazard pile.

Kaine followed Harper, who walked into a bedroom that was painted pale green with darker green accents. He was surprised it was her room; it seems to have very little of her personality. His bedroom at his house had more of her personality it in than this.

Turning, she let him unzip her dress before she stripped off. "Sera decorated it when I was gone, and I never thought to change it. All the rooms have a color theme now. It's supposed to be called the green room, but it's mine, so it's my room."

"I thought you were in France years ago?" He watched her. He had missed seeing her body all week.

"I was. I've just never had the heart to tell her I don't like it. As long as she is happy, I can live with it." Shrugging, she pulled on jeans, ones he had seen dozens of times.

"I think she'd be happy, even if you changed your room." He pulled off his jacket and tie and sat on the edge of her bed.

"Maybe." Harper pulled on her yellow "Yalling Stan" shirt over her naked breasts, and instantly, he missed them. She was completely dressed down, but her hair and makeup were still perfect.

"She isn't that delicate, is she?" He grabbed her hand and pulled her onto his lap.

"No, not at all. Nothing like that." She came willingly and nuzzled into his neck, her hands pulling his shirt from his pants until she was touching skin. "The truth is that we've spent years not wanting to spook her. See, when Dad left, they had only been married for a few weeks, and she could have walked away and never looked back. For years, she was the only thing that kept us out of foster care."

She pulled back and bit her lip at the admission.

"I think it has backfired; she isn't leaving you. Even she admits she doesn't want to leave you girls."

"We know that now. We have to push her out. Harrison is taking her away from us." She smiled despite her words.

"She will always be your mom, no matter what happens. Mabel is now married, and she's moving out. I'm hoping you will move out too."

"And give up this? *Really?*" she waved her arms dramatically around the room she had admitted she didn't even like. If he hadn't been holding onto her, she would have slid off his lap.

Suddenly, there was a knock on the door. "Stop having sex. Movie starts in five."

"Only Maby would do movies as her reception." Harper let his comment slide as she slid off his lap.

Following her out the door, he saw that Lucy was the one who was telling everyone about the movie. Downstairs, he found that Agatha and Buzz had already taken a spot on the couch, along with more alcohol than he thought imaginable.

"I'll make something, any requests? And how about fewer bottles of booze out here?" Harper grabbed a case of beer and two bottles of wine as she headed to the kitchen.

"Anything," Buzz said. "But make enough for Mom, Harrison, and the girls. They will be here soon enough."

"Maybe Aunt Arabella and Aunt Becca too," Agatha said from the couch.

"Arabella and Bex," Kaine said. Only Arabella called her Becca.

"I think Aunt Arabella and Uncle Bex." Lucy flopped onto the couch next to Buzz, cracking open a beer as she did.

"No, aunts, but do they get their own honorific? Should it be Aunt Arabella and Bex, or is Bex an aunt-in-law? Which sounds like we are forced to accept Bex instead of just her being a part of the family?" Agatha pulled a blanket over her and curled under it.

"Maybe we were better off when we had no relatives. It was easier," Harper said as she grabbed two more bottles of wine from the coffee table and took them back to the kitchen.

"Where is Maby when I have grammar questions?" Agatha demanded.

"Where are Maby and Cliff?" Kaine asked the two in the living room.

"Consummating the marriage, I would assume," Agatha stated and pretended to throw up.

"Again." Buzz giggled.

"You can only consummate once, Buzz," Harper said from beside him as she grabbed a bottle of beer from the coffee table and opened it, only to hand it to him. "After that, it's just sex."

"I think it's always just sex. A special name means nothing," Agatha argued from under the blanket.

"What special name do you have for sex, Uncle Kaine?" Buzz giggled. Agatha gagged again from her corner of the couch.

Not mentioning that she had actually said his name, nor acknowl-edging what she had asked, he kept silent. No need to tell anyone about his sex life, no matter what the others said.

"Hot, Buzz. It is called hot," Harper answered for him as she left for the kitchen, this time empty-handed.

"It probably takes hours since Harper has to tell him what to do. She can't let go of control," Agatha commented.

"I like to be in control also," Kaine told her, which only made the entire room laugh at him. That's when he realized he had walked right into the joke.

Turning, he followed the Lovely sister he was interested in. He found her digging around in a huge commercial-grade fridge. In fact, the entire room was a commercial kitchen. It was all shiny and clean.

"Nice kitchen," he said to her.

"What do you want? I have a roast, but I always have chicken," she asked him, still in the fridge.

"Roast maybe since you always make chicken."

"You're right. Something special for the wedding." She pulled out a wrapped package of meat and tossed it on the counter.

"Your kitchen is very nice," he repeated, knowing it was an impor-tant room to her, even more than her bedroom was. No way would she let Sera design this room not to her liking.

"Thanks. You paid for it. It really turned out great." She looked around it as she added a few bags of vegetables to the island with the meat.

"This is what you used the money on? All of it?" He looked around again, taking it all in.

Harper opened a bag of carrots, washed them quickly, and dumped them on the island. Looking up, she explained, "That and the seven grand we had saved. Now we can get more work and grow the company. The kitchen was holding us back."

"Or you can just work the same amount of time in a nice kitchen," he said, reminding her that they both had to make an effort.

"I don't know, Kaine. I've worked hard to get where we're at now. I would hate to just give up on it." She waved the knife she had just grabbed from a drawer at him, then started cutting up the carrots loudly.

"Maybe Lucy can do more. She seemed to do okay while you were living with me." He watched her hands as he said it. She was fast.

She stopped cutting and shook her head at him. "No, Lucy was overworked, and I can see that now. I'm never going to let her do that again. She worked too hard and didn't tell me. And anyway, we made an agreement that either both of us work another job, or neither one of us does."

"So, you're getting another job?" He moved closer to her as her cutting started again in earnest.

"I'm looking, but I haven't found anything yet. There haven't been any openings for a personal assistant from four until noon. Except that my boss was a bit …" She shrugged and started tossing the carrots in a bowl.

"Awesome?" he provided and spun her around, trapping her against the counter, touching her from chest to knees.

"Maybe not that." She giggled and used her wet hands to drag him even closer to her.

"That hurt, Harper." He nipped her neck, not even pretending not to smell her as he did.

"Break it up. This is a kitchen that has yet to be sullied by someone having sex in it," Lucy said, pushing them apart as she walked through the room to grab a bag of candy from a cabinet behind them.

"Nobody said there were new rules on sex in the kitchen." Buzz was right behind her with an empty bottle of wine, which had still been sealed when he had been in the room.

"There are rules, Buzz." Harper held him tight, glaring at her sister.

"Rules are made to be broken." Buzz shrugged and headed out of the room.

"What rules?" Clifton Scott V asked. He was in sweatpants and a T-shirt that said *"Property of Mabel Lucie Scott V"* on it.

"No sex in the kitchen," Harper stated.

"Oh, that one. I would never break that rule. Ever." He pulled his blushing bride into his arms and nuzzled her neck. The woman was red from her hairline to the top of her T-shirt that said *"If lost, return to Clifton Scott V."*

"Oh, for fucks sake, people. No sex in the common areas. What if the two littles saw you?" Harper demanded.

"They were at school," Cliff stated, then went back to messing with his new bride's hair, which was no longer in the fancy style it had been in just an hour before.

"It's summer vacation." Lucy gave him a flat look as she started washing the uncut carrots from the island—the ones her sister already washed.

"Shit," Cliff whispered, his movements stopping.

"It isn't, you idiot. I'm working, so it's not summer," the teacher reminded him with a laugh.

"You are out of my wedding, Lucy. Cut out completely," Cliff stated loudly.

"Too late. What else do you have?" Lucy set the clean carrots back where they had been.

"Don't worry; it was sullied way before it was even complete." Agatha came into the room, blanket wrapped over her shoulders.

"You?" Harper demanded.

"I wish. Nope, Mom. Couldn't you see the ass prints in the dust?" Agatha grabbed a bag of chips as all the sisters groaned.

"I just hope she got slivers, both of them. I think I'm getting a migraine." Harper grabbed her head.

"Can someone tell me right now why everyone is in the kitchen, not across town celebrating a damn wedding?" the woman herself yelled at the room. Her dress was still on, but her shoes were gone. Her fiancé followed closely, as did their kids.

"Only if you can tell me you haven't had sex in this kitchen since I paid my hard-earned money to make it nice," Harper demanded.

His sister instantly stopped talking. Her mouth was set as she crossed her arms. "Talk to my lawyer." She pointed over her shoulder, and Harrison's expression made the entire room break down laughing. The woman had thrown him under the bus.

Cliff took pity on them and put an arm around Sera. "I told them we couldn't party there, Mom Lovely. We had to party at the Lovely house. You must understand, this is our place."

"Why did you even want a wedding?!" she demanded and pushed his arm off her.

"For you," Mabel admitted quietly. Kaine remembered what Harper had said in her bedroom, that they did things for Sera because they didn't want to say no. But an entire unwanted wedding? Wouldn't someone say no to all that?

"How did you want to get married?" Sera demanded.

"On a beach in Florida. Where I fell in love with her. At sunset, with just our close friends and family there." Cliff kissed the top of his wife's head.

"And I got in the way of it? Why didn't you just say?" Sera had big tears in her eyes.

"We kind of did, but you wanted the big wedding. The doves and everything else," Mabel stated.

"Come on, Sera. Let's change and have fun, just like the bride and groom want to. Next time it's your wedding, and we will do everything you want to do." Harrison pulled her away from the group as tears ran down her cheeks.

"Good job, Maby. You made Mom cry!" Buzz barked at her sister.

"I tried not to. For weeks," Mabel stated quietly.

"Stop yelling at the Mrs., Buzz, or I will not show you the house I purchased for the love of my life as a wedding gift." Cliff picked up his sniffling bride, whose expression instantly switched from sad to surprised.

"You bought her a house?" Lucy demanded in belief.

"You bought me a house?" her twin also demanded at the same time.

"Of course, dear, we can't live with your mother forever, and the apartment isn't us. I saw one over by Kaine's place I thought would be perfect for you," Cliff told Maby.

"Can we go look?" Lucy asked, and Buzz agreed.

"The limo is still available," Agatha stated with a grin.

Buzz squealed and ran up the stairs, yelling that they were taking the limo to the new house. Within minutes the house was empty since Sera had missed the limo ride to the house, and she was not missing this one. That left Harper, who was making a meal, and Kaine because he wasn't leaving her.

"You're missing seeing the new house." He lifted her onto the countertop the moment the roast was in the oven.

"I'll see it one day. Today I get to be alone with you." Her legs wrapped around him.

"Are we having sex in your kitchen?" He liked the idea, seeing how everyone else had done it already.

"No, I worked hard to get this kitchen perfect."

"You sort of paid for it by having sex, so maybe we should just have sex in it." Kaine ran his hands up under her shirt and cupped her bare breasts.

"Are you seriously going to go there?" she demanded but didn't push him away.

"It was the best decision of my life. You are the best mistress I could have ever asked for."

"Is that all you see me as? Sex?" she giggled as he lifted the shirt over her head.

"No, you're the woman I plan to spend the rest of my life with. Getting to have sex with you is just part of it. One of my favorite parts." He kissed down her body as he unbuttoned the jeans, sliding the zipper down. All with no protest from her.

"How is that going to work? Same setup as before?" She pulled his shirt over his head.

"Nope, completely different. We will spend every hour we can together, both of us taking more time off. And I will redo my kitchen so you can work from there sometimes." She lifted her butt so that he could pull the jeans from her body, leaving her in silver panties, or what were called panties but covered nothing.

"I need to work at least five nights a week, possibly six." She held up five fingers.

"Three." He bent down two of her fingers, then kissed the three still up.

"Four." She hissed in a breath as he kissed her thighs just above the knee.

"Three, no more." He kissed up her leg.

"Four." She repeated, then groaned as he kissed back down her leg, away from where she wanted him.

"Three." He kissed up once more.

"Lucy can't do it." She moaned and threw her head back as he nipped at her tender skin, inches from her barely covered core.

"Lucy will cut back too. Maybe she can find a different second job. Something better." He felt her legs go around him, pulling him closer to her.

"I need a second job," she reminded him, and her body shivered in anticipation as his lips drew closer.

"You'll be married to a billionaire, Harper. You don't need to work at all," he said, knowing there was no way he was not marrying this woman. And soon. Yesterday if possible.

"Marry?" She sat up a little at the word, and their eyes met.

"Marry me, Harper." He watched her brown eyes as his tongue slid across her core.

"Fuck yes!" She buried her hands in his hair and wrapped her legs around his head.

Even as he was making her come with his mouth, his hands were busy getting rid of his pants—he needed to be inside her. Her orgasm hadn't stopped before he buried himself into her heat, and his mouth claimed hers. Before he had finished, they had found their way to the floor with her on top.

Though he knew others had had sex in this room, he knew none were as good as him as Harper had been.

CHAPTER THIRTY-TWO

"Leave the shirt untucked," Harper said as she handed him his dress shirt, wishing she could tell him to leave the shirt altogether. Except then everyone would know that they'd had sex, not that they wouldn't all think it anyway.

"Why?"

"Then I can touch you if I need to."

"Will you need to?"

"One never knows." She pretended to do something in the fridge to get her mind off touching him. "Did you say something about getting married?"

He grinned. "I did, and you agreed."

"I'll still have my own business, Kaine. I just can't quit."

"I'm not asking you to. But you could stop taking a salary and not get another job," he said.

"So, I won't get paid anymore? Why am I working then?" Slamming the fridge shut after grabbing nothing, she rolled her eyes at him. His plan made no sense.

"Because you love the work more than you do money."

"I guess, but Lucy won't be happy."

"She seems like she'll go with the flow. Can we try?"

He was right. All month, Lucy had stepped up when needed with no complaint, just like with everything in her life. With Harper not working, Lucy could look at getting a day job, like she herself had had, only during the day. Lucy could do that now.

"I guess, if that's what you want." He gave in. He hated to lose the argument, but he was right.

"You're what I want, Harper Lovely, or whatever name you're going by now," he teased her.

By the time the limo returned, the roast was nearly done, and she had cleaned the entire room with Kaine's help, as if he was any good at cleaning. But he looked good as he tried, and she got to touch him because his shirt was untucked.

Soon, the room was completely full of people who were discussing the disgustingly large house Cliff had bought for Mabel. It had a library, which was all she really wanted, but it also had six thousand more square feet of stuff everyone was talking about.

Once everyone had food, the table was completely full. With the addition of Harrison, Cliff, and Kaine, it was more than the table could hold, no matter how much squeezing was done. So, Harper and Kaine stood as they ate.

Lucy was the first one to finish eating; she seemed to be off today. But her sister married her best friend, which was not something that happened every day. Lucy loaded her plate in the dishwasher as Harper asked quietly, "You okay?"

"Yes, never better. Great day. How are you?" Lucy was lying, but Harper wasn't going to push her about it today, especially with everyone in the room.

"Good, I think. I might be moving in with Kaine," she whispered, not wanting everyone to hear. But Kaine did because he looked at her with a grin.

"Might? Do it! Boss sex all the time. I want boss sex." Lucy moaned as if she would ever actually sleep with her boss.

"Grow up. He isn't my boss anymore."

"Just plan sex sounds boring. Maybe you need to find a new boss. For boss sex." Lucy chuckled at her joke.

"Quit it. Now, I'm not getting another job."

"What? We either both work, or neither of us work," Lucy stated, as if her sister hadn't just said she was moving in with a billionaire. It seemed that rules were rules.

"I'm not going to take a salary, so I'm working for free until we take off, and you can quit your second job also. Hopefully, we'll get more business at The J, but besides that, we're getting busier all the time," Harper explained.

Lucy shrugged. "I guess that might work."

"You should find something other than cleaning. Something that pays more, now that you have a diagnosis," Harper said. Lucy was learning to live with her disability, so a better job was something she could do now.

"Yeah, I'll look into it," Lucy mumbled and yelled something to Cliff about buying her a house, making their conversation over. Lucy headed back towards the table.

"So, Sera, when are you moving out?" Buzz asked. Sera hadn't moved out yet, nor really packed to move in with him.

"We're looking for a place; we just haven't found it yet." Sera hedged her answer. Because the truth was, she hadn't liked anything, while Harrison loved everything. Harper assumed it was because Sera wanted Harrison to move into the house with her, not find something else.

Agatha picked at her meal. "Have you looked at the Tudor down the street?"

"Which one?" Sera asked with interest. Way too much interest.

"Two blocks down. The white one that looks haunted?" Buzz asked.

"I don't want to look at a haunted house," Violet stated loudly.

"It's not haunted. It's just been lived in by idiots. You should look, then you could still be close," Agatha stated. She knew what was happening in the neighborhood since she didn't leave it much, and she also knew what Sera needed to get her ass out of the house and in with her future husband.

"But not to Maby and Harper; they are moving out," Lucy stated, pulling a cake from the fridge.

"Where is Harper going?" Sera asked, looking at Harper with raised eyebrows.

"To live with the ass. Sorry, Mom, I mean your great brother. It seems that they're officially shacking up," Lucy answered for her.

"I get her room!" Buzz stated, louder than anyone else.

"I thought you wanted my room?" Maby asked, a little put out.

"Cliff hasn't been sneaking into Harper's," Buzz stated, looking right at her new brother-in-law, who just laughed at her.

"I haven't said I'm moving out," Harper added to the group discussing her as if she wasn't even there.

"See, man? When you find a Lovely lady, you have to tie her down. When are you marrying her?" Cliff jumped in.

"No idea," he said, not denying it at all.

"How about Christmas? A big Christmas wedding. I would love a Christmas wedding!" Sera clapped her hands in excitement.

"You're having a Halloween wedding, minus the Halloween stuff," Agatha reminded her with a groan.

"But now I can plan a Christmas one! Can you just see the cathedral with all the decorations?" she asked Harper.

"No Cathedral," Harper said maybe a little too loudly, but she had to start drawing the line now. Sera tended to go overboard quickly.

"How about something small, and then a reception at the J? Harper loves it there," Kaine said, obviously swept up in his sister's plans.

"I can work with that," Sera replied, her mind already running through ideas.

"We don't really have to have it at Christmas, so what about just doing it in a few weeks?" Kaine wrapped his arms around her. Did he know he was being roped into this by his own sister? Did he even see the trap for what it was? A damn trap!

"Another quick wedding? You kids are going to be the death of me. I'll start making arrangements," Sera said, pulling out her phone.

"Did you even propose?" Harper asked him, his arms still tight around her. "While not fucking me at the time?" she whispered, except based on Agatha's gagging sounds, she'd heard.

"Nope, I only ask when you are guaranteed to say yes. And I know how to make you say yes and my name all at the same time, over and over again." He kissed her ear, then sucked the lobe into his warm mouth, causing a shiver to run down her spine.

"Get a room!" Buzz yelled just as something solid hit Harper in the head.

Pulling away from Kaine, she touched her head and looked at the spoon clattering on the floor at her feet.

"You threw a *spoon* at me?"

"Stop making out with my uncle! My eyes can't take it." Buzz threw a fork this time, but Kaine swept her into his arms and dodged the utensil.

"I think we should leave, so nobody gets hurt." Kaine glared at the redhead.

"Uncle Chicken!" she said and was trying to take Emma's fork from her hand, but Emma wasn't having it.

"Buzz, leave them alone." Sera reached over and grabbed the fork from Emma and used it to point at Harper and Kaine. "You must stay for a wedding meeting."

"Take her and run, man. Wedding meetings are the worst," Cliff stated, earning him a glare from his new mother-in-law.

Sera tossed a bun at Cliff, hitting him in the shoulder. "At least with Harper marrying my brother, I will like one of my sons-in-law!"

Cliff held a hand to his chest. "Direct hit, Mom."

Harper wrapped her arms tightly around Kaine as he backed away from the table. She realized something new about having him around —he was going to be protective of her. He might not be able to stop her from starting something with her sisters, but he would save her when she did.As the battle continued without them, Kaine retreated even further from the table and into the empty living room. She buried her head in his neck. "Are you sure you want to be a part of this?"

She could feel him laugh as he nuzzled her hair, reminding her that she still had it up from the wedding. "I can't get out now even if I wanted to."

She pulled away and looked at him. "Because of Sera?"

"Because of you, Harper. I don't want the life I had before you moved into my house. I want the life you bring with you."

"Words like that make me wet," she whispered.

He grinned. "I thought only money did that?"

Harper laughed at his words, remembering saying that a month before. Oh, how wrong she had been about him. How wrong she had been about everything. "Money and you, babe. Just money and you."

EPILOGUE

"I THINK Sera is secretly happy that I'm marrying Kaine. That way, she can be in all the photos on both sides of the family," Harper whispered to Buzz as she took a few minutes to drink something to keep her hydrated. She hoped whiskey had that ability because she needed alcohol to get through that day.

Sera had spent more time getting her picture taken with her siblings than her kids. Harper was sure Sera was waiting for her wedding for those since all the girls would be dressed the same, except Agatha. Her mom liked a good matchy-matchy picture.

Harper had gotten to see the three together for the first time today and had to admit she should have noticed how much they all looked alike. Though Arabella and Sera were near twins, Kaine wasn't that far off. In her defense, she had no idea that there were more Seras in the world. So, she hadn't exactly been on the lookout for a male version of the woman who had raised her.

"Secretly? There was nothing less hidden. Did you even get a picture of you and Kaine alone?" Buzz handed her a bottle of cold water.

"I just hope that she enjoys her weddings," Harper mused as the woman whirled through the room on her way to the kitchen to make sure Lucy was getting everything done. Harper was forbidden from that room today, not that it had stopped her from checking up on the food a few times. What could Sera do? Ground her?

"Her wedding isn't for two weeks." Buzz watched her also, then turned back to Harper.

Sera had chosen charcoal black as the colors for Harper and Kaine's wedding. *Charcoal* black, not just black. There was no arguing once she had chosen it, and Kaine had learned that his sister got her way. Every time.

"They are all her weddings, Buzz. Even yours will be." Harper touched Buzz's chin and turned her head left end right, making sure her makeup was perfect.

Buzz pushed her hand away and stated, "I am not getting married. This is crazy. I am eloping. No way is Mom in charge of my wedding."

Touching her cheek again, she tapped Buzz on the nose. "You are so cute when you think you're different than all your sisters."

"I am different ... and slightly better." She again swatted at Harper's hands and then took a step back.

"It's the red hair. It makes you delusional." Harper followed, touching the hair that was exactly how she had wanted it. Since Buzz was her only bridesmaid, it went to reason that Harper got to dress her.

Another swat and another snarl. "When is this wedding happening? I am so tired of you."

"Not soon enough." Harper was a ball of energy, just waiting to get it over with.

Buzz walked across the room and glared at Harper, daring her to follow. "I am eloping, I mean really eloping. Not just having Cliff show up in the middle of the night with a judge, though it's turning into my favorite part of these weddings. This time, I didn't even get a parking ticket. Remind me to force that out of Cliff; he is a billionaire, after all."

"That wasn't planned. Cliff and Maby just showed up." Harper looked into the mirror to make sure every hair was in place still, which it didn't dare not be.

The night before, at slightly after midnight, Cliff and Maby showed up, followed closely by the other three sisters to do what Cliff said was "a Lovely wedding." Which was just him dragging some judge that his dad had dirt on out in the middle of the night. His only job was to marry the happy couple hours before they would stand in front of their closest family and friends to do it all over again.

Harper wasn't happy, and it wasn't welcome, not that Cliff could be stopped. He even had Arabella and Bex come over to witness the impromptu vows. Arabella was so excited and miserable at the same time that Harper was sure she would go into labor before the actual wedding today. So far, the twins were staying put. Bex, on the other hand, was grumpy, miserable, and had to be a witness to Harper and Kaine getting married not once but twice. As she signed her name as a witness, she told everyone in the room she was sure it wouldn't last.

The only good thing was that Harper had half planned it since she knew Cliff and his ways. After he had married Maby in a similar ceremony, Harper had suspicions about him pulling it on her and Kaine. And she loved being right.

Sera was the only one not invited since she would be pissed about it. After all, she had planned their entire actual wedding.

"It seemed like you were ready for it." Buzz folded her arms, thus wrinkling her dress.

Rolling her eyes at her sister's words and actions, she said, "Cliff said something that tipped me off."

"What?" The redhead raised an eyebrow.

"He told me to not be too sexed up after midnight." She grinned. That had been the hardest part of the night.

"Not really very covert, is he?"

"It's Cliff, not Maby. I let it happen; it's tradition." She shrugged.

"Kaine was very into it when he found out he was getting to marry you early. It was like he was told he could open a Christmas present the night before Christmas." Buzz shook her head.

"That happened after you left. Have I ever told you how excruciatingly slowly he unwraps presents?" Harper wiggled her eyebrow.

"No details, please!"

"What kind of details?" Bex asked as she slipped into the spare room in her dark gray suit. She had announced that if Arabella was getting a new dress, she was getting a new suit. In reality, nobody seemed to care that it was new, which pleased Harper just a little bit.

"Their sex life," Buzz stated.

Over the last few weeks, they had gotten together with Arabella and Bex a few times, but she and Bex still didn't get along. Not that either of them even tried for their spouses. Maybe one day they would be okay, but it didn't matter.

"Gross, keep it to yourself. I do not need any details about Kaine in bed. Or you, for that matter." Bex pointed at Harper. "I was sent to make sure that you were, in Kaine's words, gorgeous still. I think you just pass, but then again, you're not my type."

"He seems to like her." Buzz touched Harper's hair, and her sister batted the hand away.

"He always has, though I thought it would end after an affair. I mean, who moves their mistress into the number one spot? I didn't see this coming." Bex leaned toward Buzz, as if she said it in confidence.

"Mistress?" Buzz turned on the woman in excitement. Outside sourcing on what everyone had suspected.

"I just worked for him. Kept his house," Harper added lamely. It was going to come out sooner or later. Apparently, on her wedding day! Because of Bex Carter!

"Okay, Nelle, tell your family what you want. You getting paid for sex probably isn't the image they want in their heads either." Bex grinned.

"Shut up, Bex!" she hissed.

"Maybe I need to go talk to my new sister-in-law about her oldest. You are the oldest, right? I am sure you are. The rest seem so much younger than you," Bex stated and hurried out of the room before Harper could stop her.

"*Mistress?*" Buzz turned to her with a grin. "I think there's a story there. A story worth publishing."

"Don't you dare, Buzz! And Kaine will kill you if you do, anyway."

"Kaine doesn't scare me. Mom does," Buzz said, but barely got the words out as Harper knocked her to the ground. *Dresses be damned!*

KAINE WAS WAITING at the end of the aisle, or what was pointed out by his sister Sera as the aisle hours before, waiting for the love of his life to show up. So far, she was ten minutes late, which would have bothered him to no end if he wasn't already married to the woman.

The impromptu wedding was something he had never imagined, but his bride seemed okay with it, so he went with it. Not that it mattered anyway since he was marrying her today, no matter what.

When Sera had asked when they were getting married, he wanted to say that day but felt that would scare everyone involved. Now two weeks later, he was sure it would not. His sister was a wedding machine at this point and would get everyone married as fast as she could.

The fact that Harper hadn't argued meant that she was as much in love with him as he was with her. There was no way there would have been a wedding if she didn't fully want it, Sera or not. She had even let the other woman make almost every decision about the actual wedding. Her only response when he asked her about it was that Sera wanted a wedding way more than Harper did.

"Where is she?" Arabella whispered beside him.

"Coming." He took her hand in his and assured her.

She had chosen a black dress that she said hid her pregnancy, but it didn't. When he had thought about who he wanted to stand up with him today, hers was the only name he could think of. A few years before, when she had married Bex, he had been beside her, so it seemed right that she was there for him.

"I was promised a short ceremony." Arabella squeezed his hand hard.

"It will be once the bride shows up."

"She was more prompt last night."

"That was more her kind of ceremony than this."

"I know. I'm glad I'm already married. I don't need a Sera wedding." The sisters were getting along well and were talking and having lunch a few times a week. Arabella had been invited to brunch the weekend before, but Kaine had told her no until after the babies were born. He had seen too many of those brunches to let his sister go while pregnant.

"She'll probably want to have you get married again, just so she can plan it." Sera had hinted to him just the day before, that since she missed the wedding, a redo was needed. He had told her no, but he was sure she hadn't listened.

"I would do it again," Arabella said, and he knew she was looking at her wife in the front pew, who was trying to keep Eddie from taking off. Mostly failing.

"Stop fawning over my executive assistant."

"She said you were moving her into marketing. She's excited. She won't tell you, but she is."

"She deserves it, but then again, I'll miss all her sex talk about my sister."

"I don't think she'll stop that exactly." Arabella grinned and looked over at her wife again.

"It's in her new contract." He suddenly checked the time and saw his bride was now twenty minutes late. He knew she had late tendencies, but he let them slide now.

Suddenly, the music started, and Buzz appeared in the doorway. She was also in gray, but in a completely different style. Kaine thought that she looked good in the dress but was sure his wife was going to look amazing when she borrowed it from her sister for an event. Maybe that was why Harper had chosen that color and style.

They had decided on one attendant each since she had so many, and he had so few, and the location in their house was too small for every Lovely. Them all being in the front would leave the chairs empty of guests.

Kaine stopped breathing when Harper stepped into the archway and looked around the room until their eyes caught, and she grinned. The white dress was so form-fitting, he longed to touch it. Her blonde hair was up in a hairstyle that was perfect, at least on one side. The other was a little off.

As she drew closer, he saw that one of her eyes was more closed than the other and had more makeup on it. He could tell she was trying not to flinch as she blinked.

Looking over at the redhead, he saw she had a bruise on her cheek, and it was getting darker as he watched.

Shaking his head, he knew his wife and her bridesmaid had spent the last twenty minutes fighting and trying to fix all the damage it had caused. Neither had actually succeeded.

When she got close enough, he pulled her close and kiss the cheek under soon to be black eye. She flinched.

"Fight?" he whispered.

"Defending your honor." She grinned.

"Was the black eye worth it?"

"It's fine. Let's get this done. There might be a little more damage for you to find tonight," She said and winked at him.

Looking her up and down, he wondered if she had done it on purpose so that he had an excuse to touch her, feel her, and love her. Right then, he knew their marriage was going to be a wild ride, and he was going to enjoy every moment of it.

The End

BUZZ FALLS for the wrong guy in Falling for his Step-Sister.
Thank you so much for reading Falling **for the Boss**.

ABOUT ME, ALIE GARNETT

I love to read and prefer a little spice in those books. I am lucky enough to live on a small hobby farm in northern Minnesota with her husband and two kids. I enjoy spending time in the pasture with my two mini horses and one fainting goat (who doesn't actually faint). When I'm not writing, I'm busy trying to do all the things I didn't get to while writing. Or maybe I wouldn't have gotten to them anyway, because its laundry, dishes and fun things like that.

ALSO BY ALIE GARNETT

<u>Indulge</u>

Craving Winter

Enticing Aurora

<u>Landstad, ND</u>

Invisible

Irresistible

Impulsive

Insuppressible

Intriguing

Imperfect

Irreplaceable

<u>The Great Lovely Falls</u>

Falling for the Single Mom

Falling for his Best Friends Sister

Falling for the Boss

Falling for his Step-Sister

Falling for his Fake Wife

Falling into a Second Chance

<u>Hart Series</u>

Seeing her Pain

Her Favor

Max Valentine is Looking at Me!

Keeping her Safe

<u>Stand Alone</u>

Romancing the Doctor